D0315643

Longmans'
Simplified English Series

A JOURNEY TO
THE CENTRE
OF THE EARTH

THE DAKIN COLLECTION
UNIVERSITY OF EDINBURGH
DEPARTMENT OF LINGUISTICS
14 BUCCLEUCH PLACE
EDINBURGH EH8 9LN

File No. ....

Shelf No. ....

Presented by ....

LONGMANS' SIMPLIFIED ENGLISH SERIES

General Editor: C. KINGSLEY WILLIAMS, M.A.

JANE AUSTEN
Pride and Prejudice*

R. M. BALLANTYNE
The Coral Island
The Gorilla Hunters

H. E. BATES
The Jacaranda Tree

EDITED BY J. A. BRIGHT
Six Short Plays

CHARLOTTE BRONTË
Jane Eyre

EMILY BRONTË
Wuthering Heights

JOHN BUCHAN
Prester John
The Power House
The Thirty-Nine Steps

WILKIE COLLINS
The Moonstone
The Woman in White

A. J. CRONIN
Hatter's Castle

CHARLES DICKENS
A Tale of Two Cities

A. DUMAS
In the Service of the Queen
The Three Musketeers

ELIZABETH GASKELL
Cranford

SIR H. RIDER HAGGARD
Montezuma's Daughter

NATHANIEL HAWTHORNE
A Wonder Book

C. S. S. HIGHAM
Pioneers of Progress

ANTHONY HOPE
The Prisoner of Zenda
Rupert of Hentzau

HAMMOND INNES
Campbell's Kingdom

JEROME K. JEROME
Three Men in a Boat
Three Men on the Bummel

CHARLES and MARY LAMB
Tales from Shakespeare
More Tales from Shakespeare

DAPHNE DU MAURIER
Frenchman's Creek
Jamaica Inn
Rebecca

HERMAN MELVILLE
Moby Dick

H. SETON MERRIMAN
Barlasch of the Guard

DOROTHY L. SAYERS
The Unpleasantness at the Bellona Club

SIR WALTER SCOTT
The Talisman

R. L. STEVENSON
Dr. Jekyll and Mr. Hyde
Kidnapped

W. M. THACKERAY
Vanity Fair

EDITED BY G. C. THORNLEY
A Book of Shorter Stories
British and American Short Stories
Outstanding Short Stories

ANTHONY TROLLOPE
The Three Clerks

MARK TWAIN
The Adventures of Huckleberry Finn
The Adventures of Tom Sawyer

JULES VERNE
A Journey to the Centre of the Earth
Round the World in Eighty Days

H. G. WELLS
The Invisible Man

STANLEY WEYMAN
A Gentleman of France

ERIC WILLIAMS
The Wooden Horse

JOHN WYNDHAM
The Kraken Wakes

* *also issued in a hard cased binding*

A JOURNEY TO
THE CENTRE
OF THE EARTH

by

JULES VERNE

ADAPTED AND REWRITTEN BY
H. E. PALMER, D. LITT.

Illustrated by Harry Green

LONGMANS

LONGMANS, GREEN AND CO LTD
48 GROSVENOR STREET, LONDON WI
RAILWAY CRESCENT, CROYDON, VICTORIA, AUSTRALIA
AUCKLAND, KINGSTON (JAMAICA), LAHORE, NAIROBI

LONGMANS SOUTHERN AFRICA (PTY) LTD
THIBAULT HOUSE, THIBAULT SQUARE, CAPE TOWN
JOHANNESBURG, SALISBURY

LONGMANS OF NIGERIA LTD
W. R. INDUSTRIAL ESTATE, IKEJA

LONGMANS OF GHANA LTD
INDUSTRIAL ESTATE, RING ROAD SOUTH, ACCRA

LONGMANS GREEN (FAR EAST) LTD
443 LOCKHART ROAD, HONG KONG

LONGMANS OF MALAYA LTD
44 JALAN AMPANG, KUALA LUMPUR

ORIENT LONGMANS LTD
CALCUTTA, BOMBAY, MADRAS
DELHI, HYDERABAD, DACCA

LONGMANS CANADA LTD
137 BOND STREET, TORONTO 2

New Edition © Longmans, Green & Co Ltd 1962

First published in this Series 1938

Twelfth impression 1961

New Edition (Revised and re-illustrated) 1962

Printed in Great Britain by
Northumberland Press Limited
Gateshead on Tyne

LONGMANS'
SIMPLIFIED ENGLISH SERIES

THIS book has been specially prepared to make enjoyable reading for people to whom English is a second or a foreign language. An English writer never thinks of avoiding unusual words, so that the learner, trying to read the book in its original form, has to turn frequently to the dictionary and so loses much of the pleasure that the book ought to give.

This series is planned for such readers. There are very few words which are outside the learner's vocabulary.[1] These few extra words are needed for the story and are explained when they first appear. Long sentences and difficult sentence patterns have been simplified. The resulting language is good and useful English, and the simplified book keeps much of the charm and flavour of the original.

At a rather more difficult level there is *The Bridge Series*, which helps the reader to cross the gap between the limited vocabulary and structures of the *Simplified English Series* and full English.

It is the aim of these two series to enable thousands of readers to enjoy without great difficulty some of the best books written in the English language, and in doing so, to equip themselves, in the pleasantest possible way, to understand and appreciate any work written in English.

---

[1] The 2,000 root words of the *General Service List of English Words* of the *Interim Report on Vocabulary Selection*.

INTRODUCTION

SCIENTIFIC possibilities, travel and exciting adventures make a mixture which is popular with many readers. *Jules Verne* was one of the first to find this mixture. There have been many writers of science-adventure stories since, but Jules Verne's books are still read with pleasure all over the world. They have been translated from the French in which he wrote them nearly a hundred years ago into many languages and have been the subject of many plays and films.

Jules Verne was born at Nantes, in France, in 1828. He studied law, but some travel stories which he wrote for a Paris newspaper caught public interest. Then he began to write the stories which made him famous.

Some readers may have seen the film of his *Round the World in Eighty Days*, written in 1873 before the motor-car was invented. In *Twenty Thousand Leagues Under the Sea* (1870) his characters sailed under the North Pole in the imaginary ship *Nautilus*. This voyage was actually made for the first time in 1958 in a real *Nautilus*.

A Journey to the Centre of the Earth was written in 1864. Is there really a world below the surface of the Earth? Can men go there and come back alive?

CONTENTS

Chapter		Page
1	The Discovery	1
2	The Secret Message	10
3	It is Madness!	20
4	To Reykjavik	30
5	Preparations	40
6	Sneffel	50
7	Going Down	61
8	"Give me One More Day"	70
9	Lower Still	81
10	Lost	91
11	A Hundred Miles Down	101
12	Terrible Danger	109
13	Saknussemm Again	122
14	In a Volcano	135
15	Out of the Volcano	143
	Questions	149

I

THE DISCOVERY

On Sunday, the 24th of May, 1863, my uncle, Professor Lidenbrock, came hurrying back to his little house in the old part of Hamburg, No. 10 Königstrasse.

Martha, our cook, thought at once that she must be very late with the dinner. I thought: " Now, there will be trouble if my uncle is hungry, for he is one of the most impatient men that ever lived."

" Mr Lidenbrock back already! " cried the poor woman in a frightened voice.

" Yes, Martha; but of course dinner can't be ready yet; it is only half-past one."

" Why has Mr Lidenbrock come home so early, then? " asked Martha.

" He will tell us that himself," I said.

"Here he comes. I must go back to the kitchen, you may ask him why he has come back so early, and tell him why he can't have his dinner just yet."

I was alone, but I did not feel ready to explain things to the impatient professor. I was just going to escape to my own little room upstairs, when the master of the house came running through the dining-room and went straight to his study.[2] As he passed me, he threw his stick into a corner and his hat on the table, and shouted to me:

" Axel, follow me! "

And before I had time to move, he called out again, in the most impatient voice imaginable:

" What! Not here yet? "

So I jumped up and followed my terrible master into his study.

[1] *Professor:* the head of a department at a university.
[2] *Study:* a room in which one person reads, writes and studies.

Otto Lidenbrock was not a bad man. But he was certainly a bad-tempered man, and very difficult to please.

He was professor at the university, and gave the lessons on geology,[1] during which he regularly lost his temper. It is not that he was worried as to whether his students worked well or badly, or whether they paid attention to what he said, or whether they succeeded or failed in their examinations. Such things as these did not worry him at all. He taught in his own way, and to please himself only. What others thought of his teaching; what others learnt from his teaching was of no importance to him.

There are many professors of this sort in Germany.

My uncle, unfortunately, found some difficulty in speaking, or at least, when he spoke in public. This is an unfortunate thing for those who speak in public. In his lessons at the university he would often stop suddenly, when some long scientific word refused to escape from his mouth. At such times the word that did come out would be some wicked and violent word. Then, of course, he would lose his temper.

Now, in geology, there are many difficult names—half Greek, half Latin; terrible names, long names; names that hurt the mouth of the speaker and the ear of the hearer.

The young men knew, of course, that my uncle had this difficulty in speaking; they were used to hearing examples of it. They liked waiting to hear examples of it, knowing what was going to happen; and when the burst of anger came, they laughed. That is probably why so many students came to listen to my uncle; they liked laughing at my uncle's bursts of bad temper better than learning all those things that he was so able to teach. Anyhow, this I can say: my uncle was a true man of science.

If you gave him any stone to examine, he would look at it and feel it, or give it a knock and listen to the sound it made, or smell it—and in every case he would tell you what it was, what it was made of, and perhaps where it came from. About six hundred sorts of stone are known today,

[1] *Geology:* the study and science of the earth's rocks—the professor is a *geologist;* adj. *geological.*

and my uncle could tell you at once which of the six hundred it was.

The greatest men of science would pay him visits. They would ask his advice on difficult questions that troubled them. He had made several discoveries of the greatest scientific importance.

This, then, was the man who called me so impatiently.

He was a tall man, thin, with a body like iron, looking more like a man of forty than of fifty. He had large eyes, and these rolled about behind his large pair of glasses; his long, thin nose made you think of the edge of a knife. Some people said that his nose was a sort of magnet,[1] and that small bits of steel would stick to it—but I can tell you that this was not true. He walked at the rate of three feet to every step, and ran at the rate of four feet to every step.

He lived in his little house in Königstrasse, in the middle of the oldest part of Hamburg. Although he was only a professor, he was fairly rich. The house was his own, and all the things that belonged to it; among these were my cousin Gräuben, a seventeen-year-old girl, his servant Martha, and myself. As my father and mother were dead and he was my uncle I lived with him and helped him in his work.

I must tell you that I am a lover of geology. I am never lonely or tired in the company of stones and rocks.

On the whole, it was possible to live very happily in this little house in Königstrasse, in spite of the impatience of the owner, for although he had a rough way of showing his love, he did love me. The fact was, he was a man who could not wait, and was in a greater hurry than nature.

When he had planted flowers in April, he used to go every morning regularly and pull their leaves so as to make them grow more quickly.

So when my uncle called me, there was only one thing to do, and that was to obey. I rushed to his study at once.

The study was quite a storehouse; every sort of stone was to be found there, perfectly arranged and named. How well

---

[1] *Magnet:* a piece of iron specially treated so that it attracts other pieces of iron: *to magnetize* = to make into a magnet.

I knew these stones! How often, instead of playing with boys of my own age, I amused myself by keeping them clean.

But when I went into the study now, I hardly thought of these wonderful stones. All my attention was given to my uncle. He was sitting in a big chair, and held a book in his hands, looking at it with the greatest admiration.

" What a book! What a book! " he cried.

I must now tell you that Professor Lidenbrock was at the same time a book lover; he was mad on the subject of books; but an old book had no value for him unless it was a book that could not be found anywhere else, or a book that nobody could read.

"What! Don't you see, then? " he went on. " It is a treasure! I discovered it this morning in an old bookshop."

" Wonderful! " I answered. But I could see no reason for being so excited about an old book with the back and sides covered with dirty yellowish leather.

" Look! " he said, asking himself questions and answering them at the same time. " Is it beautiful enough? Yes, of course it is. Is it in good condition? Yes, it's in perfect condition. Does it open easily? Yes, it lies open at any page. It opens and shuts perfectly. And yet it is six hundred years old! "

All the time he was speaking, my uncle kept opening and shutting the old book. I felt that I must say something about it, although I did not feel the least interest in it.

" And what is the name of this wonderful book? " I asked.

" It's name? " he answered, with more excitement than before. " It's name is *Heims Kringla*, by Snorre Turleson, the famous Icelandic writer who lived six hundred years ago. It is the story of the Norwegian princes who governed Iceland."

" Indeed! " I said, doing my best to appear excited. " And it is written in German, of course? "

" In German! " cried the professor. " No, of course not. It is the book as it was first written, in Icelandic—that grand old language."

" Oh, I see," I answered. " And is it well printed? "

" Printed? Who is talking of printing? So you suppose this was printed, you fool! It was written by hand, and in Runic letters, too."

" Runic? "

" Yes. Don't you know what that means? Do you want me to explain that word? "

" No, of course not," I answered.

But my uncle went on with his explanations, telling me all about things that I did not want to know.

" The Runic letters were once used in Iceland, and it is said that they were invented by the gods. Look at them! Admire them! Look at these letters invented by gods! "

At that moment a dirty old parchment[1] slipped out of the old book and fell to the ground.

My uncle jumped at it, as you may easily suppose. A parchment of great age, shut up in an old book, perhaps for many hundreds of years, must seem to him to be of great value.

" What is this? " he cried, carefully putting on the table a piece of parchment five inches long and three inches wide, on which the following strange letters were written:

```
ᛒ.ᛧᛚᛂᛓᛑ      ᛏᛐᛑᛂᛐᛂᛐ      ᛐᛏᛏᛃᛒᛤ
ᛐ ᛃᛂᛐᛐᛑᚠ     ᛐᛧᛏᛐᛃᛂᚠ      ᛧᛁᛏᛤᛧᛆᛤ
ᚠᛐᛐᛃᛏᛧ       ᛁᛏᛧᛁᛐᛐᛐ       ᛐᚾ ᛊᛤᛧᛧ
ᛏᛐᛏᛧᛁᛐᛁ      ᛧᛐᛁᛐᛃᛐ        ᛧᛧᛁ ᛧᛐᛐ
ᛁᛐᛐᛐᛧ         .ᛧᛐᚦᛒᛓ        ᛁᛐᛐᛒᛐ
ᛏᚦᛤᛧᛃ        ᛐᛐᛐᛐᛐ         ᚠᛧᛐᛒᛐ
ᛤ᛭ᛐᛐᛐ        ᛤᛐᛐᛒᛒ         ᛧᛐᛤᛁᛁᛂ
```

The professor looked at these letters for some minutes and then said:

" It is Runic! These marks are exactly like those in the book. But what can they mean? "

As Runic seemed to me to be an invention of clever men to worry people who already have too many worries, I was not sorry to see that my uncle could not understand it.

[1] *Parchment:* fine sheep's skin prepared for writing.

" Yes, it is Old Icelandic! " he said to himself.

Of course Professor Lidenbrock knew that it was Old Icelandic, for he was known to be a wonderful master of languages. Not that he could speak the two thousand languages used in the world, but he knew a good deal about most of them.

A difficulty like this, then, was sure to wake up all the impatience in his nature, and I was just expecting another burst of bad language, when two o'clock struck, and Martha opened the study door and said:

" The dinner is on the table."

My uncle's answer was a violent burst of bad language.

Martha ran off, and I ran after her, and soon found myself at my usual seat in the dining-room.

I waited a few minutes. The professor did not come.

This was the first time that I had ever known him to be late for the important business of dinner. And what a dinner, too! A wonderful dinner. And this my uncle was going to lose for the sake of an old parchment. So I did my best to eat my uncle's dinner as well as my own.

" I never saw anything like this before! " cried our good Martha. " Mr Lidenbrock not to come to dinner! I can't believe it! I'm afraid something terrible is going to happen."

My idea was that the only terrible thing that might happen would be the burst of temper from my uncle when he found that his dinner had been eaten by somebody else.

I was just finishing my meal when a voice like thunder called me away from the table. I flew into the study.

" It is, of course, Runic," said the professor, " but there is a secret in it, and I will discover the secret, or else——"

He finished what he was saying with violent words and movements.

" Sit down there," he added, pointing to the table, " and write."

I was ready in a moment.

" Now, then, I am going to read out to you each modern letter which stands in the place of one of these Icelandic letters. We shall see what that will give us. But take care you don't make any mistake! "

My uncle began to read out the letters. I did my best. Every letter was called out one after another, and in the end I had before me the following strange groups of words:

mm.rnlls	esreuel	seecJde
sgtssmf	unteief	niedrke
kt,samn	atrateS	Saodrrn
emtnaeI	nuaect	rrilSa
Atvaar	.nscrc	ieaabs
ccdrmi	eeutul	frantu
dt,iac	oseibo	KediiY

When I had finished it, my uncle roughly took the paper from me and looked at it carefully for a long time.

"What can it mean?" he asked again.

I could not tell him. Besides, he did not ask me; he was speaking to himself.

"It is what we call a cryptogram,[1] where the meaning is hidden by mixing up the letters. So to make sense they must be put into their proper order. Perhaps here we have the explanation of some great discovery! "

My idea was that there was no sense in it at all, but I was wise enough not to say so.

The professor took up the book and the parchment again and compared them.

"The two were not written by the same person," he said. "The cryptogram was written a long time after the book. Here is something that proves it. The first letter stands for *mm*, which you will not find in Turleson's book, for it was not used until long after the time when Turleson lived. So there are at least two hundred years between the book and the parchment."

This seemed to be quite reasonable.

"So I suppose that these strange letters were written by somebody to whom the book belonged. But who was it?

[1] *Cryptogram:* secret writing in which the letters are mixed up in a certain way so as to hide the meaning.

Could he have put his name, I wonder, in any part of the book?"

And then my uncle began to examine carefully the first pages of the book. On the back of the first page he discovered something that looked like a dirty mark. But on examining it more closely, some letters were to be seen. My uncle saw at once that this was the chief point of interest. He looked at it again and again under his glass, until at last he was able to see that these marks were Runic letters, and these he copied out clearly.

ᛚᛆᛕᛏ ᛋᛏᛒᛐᛋᛋᛏᚼ

"Arne Saknussemm!" he cried. "Why, that is a name, and an Icelandic name, too; the name of a famous man of science who lived three hundred years ago."

I looked at my uncle with a feeling of admiration.

"These learned men," he went on, "were the only true men of science of their times. They made discoveries which may well surprise us. Why should not this Saknussemm have hidden in this cryptogram the secret of some surprising discovery? It must be so! It is so!"

"No doubt," I answered; "but what reason could this man have for hiding a wonderful discovery?"

"Why? Why? Ah, I don't know. Besides, we shall soon see. I will get the secret of this parchment, I will neither eat nor sleep until I find it out."

"Oh!" thought I.

"Nor you either, Axel!"

"Dear me!" I said to myself. "It is a good thing I have had a dinner for two today."

"The first thing to be done," said my uncle, "is to find the language of this cryptogram."

I listened. My uncle went on.

"Nothing is easier. In this paper there are 132 letters, in which there are 79 consonants[1] and 53 vowels. Now this

[1] *Consonant.* The vowels are *a,e,i,o,u.* All the other letters are *consonants—b,c,d,f,* etc.

is just about what we expect to find in the words of languages of the south of Europe, while the languages of the north have a larger number of consonants. For this reason I believe it is written in a southern language."

All this seemed very reasonable.

"But what language is it?"

It was this I waited for him to tell me, for I knew that he was very clever at this sort of reasoning.

"This Saknussemm," he went on, "was a learned man, and if he did not write in Icelandic, he would be certain to write in a language that was in common use among all men of learning at that time; I mean Latin.[1] If I am mistaken, I can try other languages. But I think that this is Latin."

I was surprised, for this group of strange and ugly words

[1] *Latin:* language of Rome spoken and written by all learned men in Europe at one time.

seemed so different from the soft and smooth language of
Rome.

"Yes, Latin," said my uncle. "But Latin all mixed up."

"Very well," I thought, "and if you can unmix it, my
dear uncle, you'll be clever."

"Let us examine it from beginning to end," he said,
taking up the piece of paper on which I had been writing.
"Here are 132 letters all in the wrong order. In some words
there are nothing but consonants, as in the first, *mmrnlls*;
others which are full of vowels—the fifth, for example,
unteief, or the last but one, *oseibo*. Now it is clear to me that
this arrangement is an accidental one. It seems to me certain
that the message was first written regularly, and then turned
upside down according to some rule that I must find out.
Anyone who has the key of the cryptogram could read it
easily. But where is the key?"

I did not answer, and for a good reason. I was looking
at a picture hanging on the wall opposite me, the picture of
Gräuben,[1] who was just now at Altona on a visit. Her being
away made me very unhappy, for—I may as well confess it
now—Gräuben and I loved each other with true German
patience and calmness. We had agreed to marry each other,
but my uncle knew nothing about the arrangement, for he
was too much of a geologist to understand such things as
love.

2

THE SECRET MESSAGE

GRÄUBEN was a pretty girl. She was fair, with blue eyes,
and rather serious in her ways. The picture of this girl whom
I loved so deeply took my mind away from thoughts of old
books and parchments, and put in their place sweet
memories.

[1] Pronounced *Groiben*.

I could see my dear companion as we worked and passed out time together. Every day she helped me to put my uncle's stones in order. Indeed Miss Gräuben was quite a geologist. She loved to examine the deepest questions of science. What pleasant hours we had spent in studying together!

And when our work was over, we used to go out for a walk beside the river as far as the end of the lake, talking all the way and holding each other's hands! I used to tell her amusing stories to make her laugh.

I was thinking of these things when I heard my uncle give a sudden blow on the table, and once more I paid attention to him.

"Look here!" he said, "it seems to me that if a man wished to mix up the letters in any message, the first thing he would think of would be to write the words up and down, instead of from left to right, in groups of five or six."

"Indeed!" thought I.

"We must see what that will do. Write some sentence on this piece of paper, but instead of putting the letters one after another, put them one under another in groups of five or six."

I understood what he meant, and at once wrote from top to bottom:

```
I  y  d  i  G  e
l  o  e  t  r  n
o  u  a  t  ä  !
v  m  r  l  u
e  y  l  e  b
```

"Very good!" said the professor, without reading what I had written. "Now arrange these words in lines."

I did so, and this was the result:

IydiGe   loetrn   ouatä!   vmdlu   eyleb

"Just so," said my uncle, taking the paper. "This has

the look of the old parchment already. Vowels and consonants are grouped in the same disorder."

I could only think that all this was most true.

"Now then," said my uncle, "I don't know what you have written, but all I need do to make it possible to read it is to take the first letter of each word one after another, and then the second, and then the third, and so on."

And to his great surprise, and certainly still more to mine, my uncle read:

I love you, my dear little Gräuben!

"What's this, what's this?" said the professor.

For really, like a fool in love, I had written this without knowing it.

"Ah! you love Gräuben," went on the professor, in a very severe voice.

"Yes—no—I mean—— Well——" I said.

"Ah! you love Gräuben," he said again. "Well, well, let us try this plan with the parchment."

My uncle was thinking only of the cryptogram, and had already forgotten the words that told him my secret.

Professor Lidenbrock's eyes grew bright as he took up the parchment with shaking fingers. He was greatly excited. At last, in a serious voice he read the following letters, calling out the first of each word, and then the second, and so on, as he had done in my unfortunate sentence:

> mmessunkaSenrA.icefdoK.segnittamurtn
> ecertserrette,rotaivsadua,ednecsedsadne
> lacartniiiluJsiratracSarbmutabiledmek
> meretarcsilucoYsleffenSnI.

I must confess that I felt excited as I came to the end. The letters themselves as they were called out one by one sounded meaningless, but I quite expected to hear my uncle read out some fine piece of Latin.

But instead of this, to my surprise, he gave a terrible blow to the table.

" That's not it! " he cried out in a voice like thunder. " It does not make sense! "

The next minute he was off, running down the stairs and away out into the street as fast as his legs could carry him.

" He has gone! " cried Martha, running up to see what the noise was, for the door was shut with such a noise that it shook the house from top to bottom.

" Yes," I answered. " He has gone."

" And without his dinner? "

" He won't have any."

" Nor supper either? " asked the old servant.

" Nor supper either," I said.

" What does it mean? " asked Martha.

" My dear Martha, he will neither eat any more nor let anyone else in the house eat."

" Oh! Then we must die for lack of something to eat! "

This seemed true, but I hardly dared tell her so.

The old servant was frightened, and went back to the kitchen with an unhappy face.

Now that I was alone, the thought came into my head that I would go and tell Gräuben about the whole business. But how could I get away? The professor might be back at any moment. And suppose he called me, and wanted to begin working again on the cryptogram. And if I were not there when he called me, what would happen?

The wisest plan would be to stay, and I had plenty to do, for a geologist in France had just sent us a large number of stones to be named. I began to work on these, examining and arranging them.

But this work did not stop me from thinking about the old parchment. I felt worried, and an uncomfortable feeling began to come over me. I had the idea that something terrible was going to happen.

After an hour's work all the stones were in their right place, and I sat down in the big chair listening and waiting for my uncle to come back. But there was not a sound. Where could he be? I seemed to see him walking with long steps along the road to Altona, among the beautiful trees, making impatient movements, cutting off the tops of the flowers with his stick, and frightening the birds.

Would he find the secret as he walked, and come back smiling and happy at his success? Or would he give up the idea of finding it, and come back unhappy, disappointed and in a bad temper? As I was asking myself these questions, I took up the paper on which I had written the groups of letters, and I said to myself:

"What can this mean?"

I tried to arrange the letters so as to form words. It was impossible. I might arrange them this way and that, putting two or three, or five or six together, but I could make no sense out of them. It is true that the 14th, 15th and 16th would make the English word *ice*, and the 84th, 85th, and 86th would make *sir*, and in the middle of the paper I noticed the Latin words *rota, mutabile, ira, nec, atra*.

"Well," I said to myself, "these last words certainly do seem to prove that my uncle is right about the language in which it is written. And in the 4th line again, I noticed the word *luco*, but on the last line I noticed the words *mer, arc, mère*, which are French.

It was enough to drive anyone mad. Three different languages in this meaningless message. I tried again and again to find sense, looking at the paper so long that the letters seemed to be flying round and round in my head. I felt that I wanted air, and began to move the paper backwards and forwards as if it were a fan. The back and the front came in sight one after another, and as they did so it seemed that I could see in the back some perfectly good Latin words, among others *craterem* and *terrestre*.

Suddenly light came to my mind. I understood. I had found the key to the cryptogram. It was not even necessary to read it through the back of the page. No, just as it was, exactly as I had written it, it could be read easily. The professor was right in the arrangement of the letters, and right about the language. One step more would make it possible for him to read the whole message, and this one step more had by accident just been shown to me.

It may be imagined how excited I was. Tears came into my eyes, and I could hardly see.

At last I managed to calm myself. I walked round the room twice, and then sat down again in the chair.

"Now, I'll read it," I said, taking a long breath.

Putting my finger on each letter one after another, I read aloud the whole.

But I was struck with fright! I sat without movement. What! Had anyone really done what I had just read? Had any man really been brave enough to do it?

"No, no!" I cried, jumping up from my chair; "I won't let my uncle know it. He would not be satisfied with just the knowledge of what had been done. He would go on the same journey himself. Nothing would stop him. Being so very interested in geology, he would start off in spite of everything, no matter what might happen. And he would take me with him, and we should never come back. No!"

I cannot describe how frightened and worried I was.

"No, no, I will not," I cried, "and as I can stop my uncle from getting such an idea into his head, I will stop him. If he began examining the paper again, turning it this way and that, he might discover the key. I'll burn it."

There was still a little fire in the fire-place. I took up both the piece of paper and the parchment of Saknussemm, and was just going to throw them on the fire, and so make an end of this dangerous secret, but at that moment the door of the study opened, and my uncle came in.

I had only time to put the papers back on the table. Professor Lidenbrock hardly seemed to notice that I was there. His thoughts had given him no rest. It was clear that he had been thinking and thinking over the matter during his walk, using all his reasoning and imagination, and he had come back to work at the secret again.

In fact, as soon as he sat down he took up his pen and began writing out fresh arrangements of the letters.

My eyes followed his hand. I noticed all his movements. What would he find? I was frightened, but I need not have been so, for as the right arrangement, and the only one, had been already found, it was useless to try any other way.

For three hours my uncle went on with his work without speaking or even raising his hand, beginning again and again a thousand times.

I knew quite well that if he succeeded in arranging all the letters in all the different ways possible, the right sentence must come out. But I knew that twenty letters only can be arranged in 2000432000090200000800117564000 different ways. Now there were 132 letters in the message, and these 132 letters would make the number of different ways so large that we should have to use very many figures if we wanted to write it down.

So it seemed to me that the professor could not get at the secret in that way.

But the time passed on and night came. The noisy street had become quiet, but my uncle, still working at the cryptogram, saw nothing, not even Martha when she opened the door and said, "Will you have any supper, sir?"

He never heard her, and the good old servant had to go away without getting an answer. As for myself, I kept awake as long as I could, but at last I felt too tired and I went to sleep in my chair, while my uncle went on with his work.

When I woke up the next morning the professor was still at work. His red eyes and white face told me how he had been fighting against the impossible.

Really he made me feel sorry for him. The poor man was so full of the one idea that he forgot to be angry. I began to be afraid that, as his bad temper could not escape in the usual way, he would finish by exploding!

I could have put an end to his trouble by one word or movement, and yet I did not. My reason was a good one. For my uncle's sake I said nothing.

"No, no," I thought, "I won't say a word. He would want to go; I know he would. He would not care about any danger to his life if he could do what no other geologist has done. I'll say nothing about it; I will keep the secret that an accident has shown me. The journey would kill him. Let him guess if he can. Anyhow, it will not be my fault if he guesses it."

Having decided, I waited. But I was not expecting something that happened a few hours later.

When Martha was ready to go out as usual to do her shopping, she found the door locked. The key of the front door was not there. Who had taken it? My uncle must have taken it when he came back from his walk the night before.

But had he taken it on purpose, or had he taken it without knowing what he was doing? Did he really mean to make us hungry? This seemed to me to be too much. Was he going to make Martha and me suffer for some reason that was no business of ours? Probably that is what he meant to do, for I remember that once before he had done something of the same sort. When he was busy writing his famous book, he ate nothing at all for forty-eight hours, and everybody in the house had to go without food too. I remember how hungry we were. It certainly looked as if we were to go without breakfast in the same way that we had to go without supper the night before. Anyhow, I decided to be brave in spite of hunger. Martha did not like the idea at all, and looked very unhappy. What worried me most was the fact that I could not get out of the house.

My uncle was still at work. He was thinking only of arrangements of letters and not of such things as resting or eating.

About twelve o'clock we began to feel really hungry. Martha had eaten up all the food that was left the night before. There was no more food at all in the house. I still tried to be brave.

Two o'clock. Waiting for food, and getting none was becoming a foolish business. It was getting too much for my patience. I began to see things in a different way. Perhaps, after all, my uncle would not believe in the message written on the parchment. Perhaps he would just laugh at it and treat it as something of no importance. Supposing even that he did treat it as something serious, what could he do? Supposing even that he wished to go on this dangerous journey, he could be stopped. I could stop him. And then again, perhaps he would discover the secret without my help. In that case I should be going without food needlessly.

These now seemed to be very good reasons to me, although the night before they had seemed to me to be no reasons at all.

I even thought that it had been foolish of me to wait so long. I decided to show my uncle the secret as soon as I could do so without seeming to do so too suddenly.

The professor got up and took his hat, and was going out.

What! Was I going to let him leave the house, and shut us all in again without food? No.

"Uncle!" I said.

He did not seem to hear me.

"Uncle Lidenbrock!" I said in a louder voice.

"What's that, what's that?" he said, like a man suddenly awakened from sleep.

"Well, have you found the key?"

"The key? What key? The key of the door?"

"No," I answered. "The key of the secret."

The professor looked at me, and no doubt noticed something unusual in my face, for he took hold of my arm sharply, and without a word looked at me again as if he were asking a question. He could not have asked me a question more clearly.

I made a movement with my head, as if to say, "Yes, I have the key."

He shook his head, as if to say, "You are a fool."

' I moved my head again. His eyes grew brighter, and he held me more tightly.

This talk of ours without words would have been interesting to anybody who had been there to see. And, really, I was now almost afraid to speak; I was afraid that in his joy he might crush me to death.

He held me more and more tightly. He began to hurt me, so I had to answer:

"Yes," I said, "this key has by accident——"

"What are you saying?" he cried, with terrible excitement.

" Here! Take this! " I answered, giving him the piece of paper on which I had written the words that he had read out to me. " Read it! "

" But there is no sense in it! " he said, ready to throw the paper away.

" No, not if you begin at the beginning, but if you begin at the end——"

Before I had time to finish what I was saying, the professor gave a cry, or rather, I should say, a roar. He had come to understand. His face had quite changed.

" Ah! clever Saknussemm! " he cried. " Your sentence was written backwards, then! "

And, taking the piece of paper, he read slowly and with a shaking voice the whole message, beginning with the last letter. It was as follows:

" In Sneffels Yoculis craterem kem delibat umbra Scartaris Julii intra calendas descende, audas viator, et terrestre centrum attinges Kod feci. Arne Saknussemm."

Bad Latin, it is true. But the meaning was clear:

" *Go down the crater*[1] *of the Yokul of Sneffel, that the shadow of Scartaris softly touches before the beginning of July, brave traveller, and you will come to the centre of the earth. Which I have done. Arne Saknussemm.*"

My uncle jumped as he read this. He jumped as if he had received an electric shock. At this moment of success his signs of satisfaction, joy and decision were wonderful to see. He went up and down the room knocking the furniture about, and—believe it or not—picking up some of his most valuable stones, throwing them into the air and catching them as they fell. At last he grew calmer and sank down in his chair.

" What time is it? " he asked.

[1] *Crater*: the mouth or opening in the middle of a VOLCANO (= mountain caused by explosion of hot rocks and gases under the earth, adj. VOLCANIC).

"Three o'clock," I answered.

"I have had no dinner! I'm dying for need of food! Let me have something to eat at once. And then——"

And then?"

"Get my big bag."

"Your big bag?"

"Yes, and pack it."

"Pack your bag? What for?"

"And pack your bag too," added the pitiless professor, as he passed into the dining-room.

These words made my heart sink, but I thought it better to give the appearance of agreement. It was certain that my uncle would listen only to scientific reasons against the journey. And there were good reasons, too. To go to the centre of the earth! What madness! Still, I would speak of these things later; my business for the present was the matter of dinner.

3

IT IS MADNESS!

I NEED hardly say how angry my uncle was when he found there was no food in the house. But we explained this to him. He gave us the key and Martha at once went off to buy things for dinner. About an hour later I was no longer hungry, and I began to think seriously of what I should say to my uncle. During the meal he was in a very good temper. He seemed quite happy and once or twice almost laughed. He even made a few jokes—something he did not often do. At the end of the meal he told me to come into his study.

I went. He sat down at one end of the table and I sat down at the other end.

"Axel," he said, in a rather gentle voice, "you are a clever fellow. You came to my help just when, tired with my efforts, I was going to give up trying. I shall never forget this, my boy."

"Well," I thought, "he is now in a good temper; this is the time to talk to him seriously."

"Above all," my uncle went on, "you must say nothing to anybody about this. There are men of science who are jealous of me. They must know nothing about it until we come back. If this message were known, hundreds of geologists would follow the road of Arne Saknussemm."

"That is just what I doubt, uncle, for there is no proof that the message is a true one."

"What! Didn't we discover it in the book?"

"Yes, and I agree that Saknussemm wrote those lines; but does it necessarily mean that he really went on that journey and reached the centre of the earth? May not this parchment be a foolish joke?"

It was perhaps rather unwise of me to use that last word. But my uncle was not angry. He simply smiled and said:

"That is what we shall see for ourselves!"

"Ah," said I, "but will you allow me to say all that is in my mind about this parchment?"

"Say all that you wish to say, my boy. Speak freely. Forget that I am your uncle. Your discovery of the secret has given you the right to speak to me as one scientist to another."

"Well, I should like to know what is meant by this *Yokul, Sneffel* and *Scartaris.*"

"I have no difficulty in telling you that. I happened only a short time ago, to get this map from a friend of mine in Leipzig. It is one of the best maps of Iceland, and it will tell us everything we want to know."

As I looked at it, the professor said:

"Look at this island and its volcanoes. You will see that they all have the name of *Yokul.* The name *Yokul,* then, is used for all the volcanoes in the island."

"Well, and what is this *Sneffel?*" I asked.

"Follow my finger along the western side of Iceland. You see Reykjavik, the chief city? Yes, well, what do you see at this point?"

" A mountain."

" Well, that is Sneffel. It is a mountain 5,000 feet high. One of the most interesting in the island, and certainly the most famous in the whole world if its crater leads to the centre of the earth."

" But that is impossible! " I said.

" Impossible? " said the professor severely, " and please tell me why."

" Because the crater must be filled up with lava,[1] and because——"

" And what if the volcano is no longer active? "

" No longer active? "

" Yes. The number of active volcanoes on the earth is only about 300, but old volcanoes are to be found in far larger numbers. Now among these is Sneffel, and the only explosion we know of took place in the year 1229. From that time the noises began to grow less and less, and now it is no longer counted among the active volcanoes."

I had no answer to make to this, so I had to pass on to the other strange word in the message.

" What does *Scartaris* mean? And what has the beginning of July to do with it? " I asked.

My uncle thought for a few minutes, and I began to hope. But only for a moment, for he soon went on again and said:

" What is darkness to you is light to me. Saknussemm was very clever. Sneffel has several craters; so it was necessary to show which of them led to the centre of the earth. He did it by saying that about the end of June, one of the mountain-tops, Scartaris, throws its shadow over the opening of the right crater. Could anyone show more exactly which road to take? "

Really my uncle had an answer for everything. I soon saw that it would be useless for me to find fault with the words of the message. So I began to point out scientific reasons against the journey.

---

[1] *Lava:* the material which flows red-hot from a volcano and cools to become very hard rock.

"Well, then," I said, "I have to confess that the message is quite clear. I will even admit that it is a serious one. Saknussemm has been to the bottom of Sneffel; he has seen the shadow of Scartaris fall over the edges of one of its craters about the end of June; he has even heard stories that this crater leads to the centre of the earth; but to believe that he got there himself, that he ever made the journey, or came back if he did—no! a hundred times no! "

"And your reason? " asked my uncle, smiling at me as if he were smiling at the foolish talk of a child.

"My reason is that science proves that such a journey could not be made."

"Science says so? " answered the professor. "Ah, what a troublesome thing science is! Isn't it a pity that science tells us that possible things are impossible! "

I saw that he was laughing at me, but I went on, all the same.

"Yes," I said. "It is well known that as you go down deeper into the earth the heat becomes greater at the rate of about one degree in 70 feet. So as it is about 4,000 miles to the centre of the earth, the heat must be about 20,000 degrees. That means that the hardest rocks and metals must be in a state of burning gas. I ask you, then, if it is possible to go to such a place."

"So it is the heat, then, Axel, that worries you? "

"Of course. Even if we went down a few miles we should find there that the heat was about 1,300 degrees."

"And you are afraid of melting? "

"I leave it to you to answer that question," I said, a little angrily.

"And I will answer it," said Professor Lidenbrock severely. "Neither you nor I nor anybody else knows anything certain about what the earth is like even one mile down. Science is always changing as new facts are discovered. What seems to be true one day is proved to be untrue the next day. Until a short time ago it was believed that as you went away from the earth the cold got greater and greater. Now we know that this is not the case. It is nowhere colder than 40 or 50 degrees below the temperature of ice. Why should it not be the same thing with heat? Why should there not be a point beyond which the heat cannot become greater?"

As my uncle was now dealing with ideas and not facts, I could say nothing to this. He continued:

"And now let me tell you this: many learned men have proved that if the temperature of the centre of the earth were 20,000 degrees, the hot gases would have such a pressure that the earth would burst."

"But that is only a belief, uncle, after all!"

"Certainly, but most geologists agree in thinking that the inside of the earth is made neither of gas nor of water, nor of the heaviest rocks and metals known, for in that case the weight of the earth would be half what it really is."

"Oh, you can make figures prove anything!"

"And facts, too, my boy. Is it not true that the number of volcanoes has been getting less since the early days of the world? And if there were great central heat, would it be likely to get less powerful?"

"If you begin supposing things, uncle, I have nothing more to say."

"And I have to say that what I suppose is what some of the most famous men of science suppose. Do you remember a visit that Sir Humphry Davy, the great scientist, paid me in 1825?"

"No, I don't remember it at all, as I only came into the world nineteen years later."

"Well, Humphry Davy came to see me, in passing through Hamburg, and among other things we talked about what the centre of the earth might be like. For a reason to which science can find no answer, we both agreed that it must be solid."

"And what is that reason?" I asked in surprise.

"It is this. If the inside of the earth were not solid, it would have tides like the sea. It would move twice a day towards the moon and away from it, and we should have violent earth movements everywhere all the time."

" And yet," I said, " the earth was once in a burning state, and we must agree that the outside got cold first."

" No," said my uncle, " the part of the earth that was in a burning state was the surface. Some metals begin to burn when they are touched by water. Well, the surface of the earth was made of these metals, and when the rain fell they would burst into fire. As the rain water went farther and farther down into the earth it would cause fresh fires, which would burst out in explosions and cracks. That is why there were so many volcanoes in the early ages."

Really, I began to think that my uncle might be right.

" You see, Axel," he went on, " geologists have always wondered what the middle of the earth is like, but they have never proved that it is burning hot. My opinion is that it is not hot; it cannot be hot. But we'll go and see, and, like Arne Saknussemm, we will find out for ourselves who is right."

" Yes, we will! " I cried, now becoming as happy and excited as my uncle. " We shall see, that is to say if we can see at all there."

" And why not? May we not expect to find some electric light? Even the pressure of the heavy air may give us light."

" Yes, it is possible, after all."

" It is certain," said my uncle. " But, remember, tell nobody about it. Let nobody try to discover the centre of the earth before we do so ourselves."

And so our talk came to an end. The excitement of it made me feel as if my head were burning. I left my uncle's study and went out of the house to get more air. But there was not enough air in the streets of Hamburg to cool me. I walked along by the side of the river.

Did I believe in the possibility of a journey to the centre of the earth, or was it that the words of the professor made me imagine the possibility? Must I take the matter seriously? Had I been listening to the mad talk of a fool or to the reasonable talk of a great man of science? What was the truth about the matter, where did the truth begin, and where did it end?

B

I certainly had believed, and at one moment I had been ready to pack my bag and start off for the centre of the earth. But in less than an hour after, this unnatural excitement had left me, and my doubts came back to me.

"It is simply madness!" I said to myself. "It is not common sense. My uncle is wrong."

I had been walking along the bank of the river, and had passed out of the town into the country. I walked in the direction of Altona, perhaps on the chance of meeting Gräuben. And indeed, it was not long before I saw her on her way home.

I called out to her.

"Axel!" she said in surprise. "Ah! you came to meet me."

But when she looked at me she saw how worried I was.

"What is the matter?" she asked, holding out her hand.

I then told her all about the matter that was worrying

me. For a minute or two she said nothing, while we walked on together. Then she said:

"Axel!"

"Gräuben," I answered.

"That will be a great journey."

I gave a jump.

"Yes, Axel, a journey worthy of a great man of science, a journey to be proud of. It is right for a man to become famous by helping in a wonderful work of this sort."

"What! Gräuben! Do you really think I ought to go?"

"Yes, Axel, I should like to go with you, but a poor girl like me would be of no help, but rather the opposite."

"Is that the truth?"

"It is the perfect truth."

Ah, those women and young girls—it is always impossible to understand them. They are either the least brave or the bravest of people. Reason has nothing to do with them. What an idea! For this child to advise me to start off on this journey, and being willing to go herself, too!

I hardly knew what to say, and I felt rather ashamed—and not quite pleased, I must confess.

"Gräuben," I answered, "we'll see if you will say the same thing tomorrow."

"Tomorrow, dear Axel, I shall say the same as today."

We walked on together, hand in hand, without saying any more. I felt quite tired by the exciting things that had been happening.

"After all," I thought to myself, "the beginning of July is not here yet, and many things may happen before that, which may make my uncle give up the idea of this underground journey."

It was late in the evening when we reached the house in Königstrasse. I expected to find everything quiet, and my uncle gone to bed, as usual.

But I had forgotten my uncle's impatience. I found him calling out and running about among a lot of men who were bringing all sorts of goods into the house. The old servant looked as if she were going mad.

"Come along, Axel! Come at once!" he called out as soon as he saw me. "You terrible fellow, you haven't started packing yet; you haven't arranged my papers; you haven't done anything!"

I stood without saying a word. I was surprised. I was more than surprised. At last I said:

"We are going, then?"

"Yes, of course we are! What do you mean by going for a walk instead of being here to help me pack?"

"We are really going?"

"Yes, I tell you. The day after tomorrow, early in the morning."

I did not want to hear any more. I could not bear any more, and rushed to my little room.

There could be no doubt about it. My uncle had spent all the afternoon in buying things needed for the journey. The ground, the tables and the chairs were covered with them. There were so many things that it would need at least ten men to carry them all.

I spent a terrible night. The next morning I heard someone calling me. I made up my mind not to open the door, but I soon found it was the soft voice of Gräuben, saying:

"Axel, dear Axel!"

I came out of my room, thinking to myself that Gräuben would change her mind when she saw my white, tired face and my eyes red for want of sleep.

But as she met me, she said:

"Ah! you are better today, dear Axel, I see. You have had a good night's rest."

"A good night's rest!"

I went to look at myself in the glass. I must confess that I did not look so bad as I had supposed.

"Axel," said Gräuben, "I have been having a long talk with Professor Lidenbrock. He is a man who is not afraid of anything, and you must be proud to think that he is your uncle. He has told me all his plans and hopes, and why and how he expects to carry out his plan. He will succeed, I am certain. Ah! Axel, it is a fine thing to be able to give one's life to science. Mr Lidenbrock will become very famous, and you will become famous, too. When you come back, Axel, you will be a man, free to speak, free to do what you like, you will be free to——"

Then she stopped, but I knew what she meant. Her words made me feel more eager, but even then I could not imagine that we were really going away. I took Gräuben with me to the professor's study.

"Uncle," I said, "is it quite decided that we are to go?"

"What! Have you any doubt about it?"

"No," I said, afraid of making him angry. "Only I want to know why we should be in such a hurry."

"Why, because of time, of course."

"But this is only the 26th of May, and between now and the end of June——"

"And do you suppose, you foolish boy, that we can get to Iceland so easily? If you had not gone out, I should have taken you to the office of the shipping company, where you would have heard that there is only one boat between Copenhagen[1] and Reykjavik, and that is on the 22nd of every month."

"Well?"

"Well, if we wait until the 22nd of June, we shall get to Iceland too late to see the shadow of Scartaris touch the crater of Sneffel. So we must get to Copenhagen as quickly as we can. Go and back your bag."

There was nothing to be said, so I went upstairs again to my room. Gräuben followed me. She put together all the things I needed for the journey. She was as calm as if I were only going to the next town. She talked quietly to me, and gave me the best reasons why it would be a good thing to go on the journey. I did not like it at all, and I felt angry at having to leave her, and I felt like telling her what I thought.

At last everything was ready, and I went downstairs.

---

[1] *Copenhagen:* English name for the capital of Denmark. Iceland was then ruled by Denmark.

During the day there came to the house more and more supplies of goods: guns, tools and scientific instruments of all sorts. Martha could not understand what was going on.

" Is the master mad? " she asked.

I made a movement with my head, meaning " yes ".

" And is he going away, and taking you with him? "

I made the same movement.

" Where to? "

I pointed with my fingers towards the middle of the earth.

" Are you going downstairs into the kitchen? "

" No," I said, at last, " lower down than that."

Evening came.

" Tomorrow morning," said my uncle, " we start at six o'clock."

At ten o'clock that evening I fell on my bed as heavily as if I were made of stone.

All through that night I dreamt. I dreamt of the professor pulling me away farther and farther into the earth. I was falling down and down the sides of underground mountains, falling quicker and quicker; it was one long, long fall that never came to an end.

4

TO REYKJAVIK

A T five o'clock I woke up. I was tired and frightened. I went to the dining-room and found my uncle already at table eating as fast as he could as many things as he could. It made me feel ill to look at him. But Gräuben was there, and I said nothing. I could not say anything. At half-past five the big carriage came to the door to take us to the railway station. It was soon packed with my uncle's luggage.

" And where is your bag? " my uncle asked.

" It is ready," I answered in a low voice.

" Make haste and bring it down then, or we shall lose the train."

I could fight no longer. I went up to my room, rolled my bag down the stairs, and followed it at once.

My uncle was saying good-bye to Gräuben. Then she turned to me.

" Go, dear Axel, go! " she said. " You are leaving me now; but when you come back, you will find your wife."

I put my arms round her, and pressed her to me, but I could say nothing except:

" Good-bye, my sweet Gräuben."

Then I took my place in the carriage. Martha and Gräuben stood at the door calling out a last good-bye, and the next moment my uncle and I were on our way to the railway station.

At half-past six we were at the station. All my uncle's luggage was taken off the carriage, marked, weighed and put on the train. At seven o'clock we took our seats, and the train was off.

I was still full of doubt and unhappiness, but the fresh morning air and the railway journey took my mind away in some degree from the longer journey on which we had started. I looked out of the window and saw the fields and woods flying past us as we made our way towards Denmark.

But the train was far too slow for the professor. It was as if his impatient thoughts were trying to make it move on faster. We were alone in the carriage, but neither of us spoke.

My uncle took everything out of his pockets and bag to make certain that he had forgotten nothing.

In three hours from the time we started, the train stopped at Kiel, close by the sea. From here we were to go to Copenhagen by boat. There was no need for us to trouble about our luggage. It would be taken off the train and put on the boat, and we should receive it at Copenhagen. But my uncle was not satisfied. Suppose that some of the luggage should be lost or forgotten! So my uncle watched every piece of luggage taken off the train, carried to the boat, and put in its right place.

My uncle had arranged things so well that we found that a whole day would be lost here, as the boat did not start until the evening. So my uncle spent nine hours in the most impatient state that you can imagine.

The nine hours came to an end at last. At ten o'clock we took our places on the boat, and a quarter of an hour later we started.

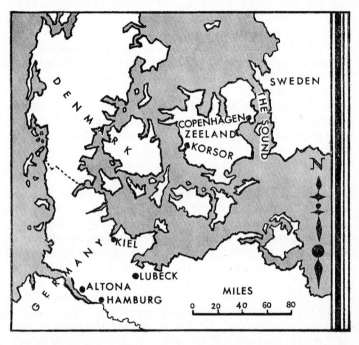

The night was dark. There was a strong wind and a rough sea. Lights could be seen here and there along the coast. That is all I remember of this part of the journey.

At seven o'clock in the morning we reached Korsor, a little town on the eastern side of Zeeland. Here we jumped into

another train, which carried us over the flat country of
Denmark. We had a three hours' journey still before reaching Copenhagen. My uncle had not slept at all. I really
believe that in his impatience he was trying to push the
carriage along with his feet.

At last he caught sight of the sea in the distance.

"The Sound!" he cried.

On our left there was a very large building. "It is a mad-
house," said one of our travelling companions.

"Well," I thought to myself, "that is a place in which we
certainly ought to end our days; but large as it is, it would
still be too small to hold all the madness of Professor
Lidenbrock."

At ten in the morning we reached Copenhagen. The
luggage was put on a carriage and we went to the hotel. This
journey took us half an hour because the station was outside the town. After a hurried breakfast the professor made
me come out with him. He wanted to go to the Department
of Geology. The man at the office of the hotel spoke German
and English, but the professor asked him in good Danish,
and it was in good Danish that the man told him the
way.

The head of this department was Professor Thomson. As
he knew my uncle by name, he received us with great kindness, showed us all the things of interest in the department,
and answered all my uncle's questions about Iceland and its
geology. Of course we said nothing to this good man about
the reason for our journey.

Mr Thomson made himself free, so that he could help us.
He went to various places trying to find a ship that would
be sailing to Iceland. I hoped that he would not be able to
find one. But he did. A small Danish ship, the *Valkyrie*, was
to start on the 2nd of June for Reykjavik. When my uncle
met the captain, Mr Byarne, he shook hands with him with
so much force that he almost cried out with pain. He was
rather surprised, for going to Iceland did not seem to him
to be at all unusual. My uncle thought it was wonderful,
and so the captain, noticing his happiness and excitement,

asked for twice the usual price for the journey. But my uncle did not mind.

"Be on the ship on Sunday morning by seven o'clock," said Captain Byarne, as he took the money.

We then went back to the hotel after giving our best thanks to Professor Thomson for his trouble.

"This is splendid! Splendid! " said my uncle. "How fortunate we were in finding a ship ready to start. Now we'll go and look at the town."

I admired everything with the pleasure of a child who sees interesting things for the first time. My uncle walked along noticing nothing except a certain high church tower on the island which forms the south-western part of Copenhagen. We went across to the island, and after going through several narrow streets, stopped in front of the church. There was nothing particularly interesting about it. But this is why the tower had caught my uncle's attention. It was more than usually high, and on the outside there were steps going round it up to the top.

"Let us go up," said my uncle.

"But it will make me unsteady. I cannot look down from high places."

"All the more reason for going. We must get used to looking down from high places."

"But——"

"Come, I tell you; do not waste time."

I was forced to obey. The man who kept the church key lived on the other side of the street. I went and got the key from him, and we began to go up.

My uncle went first. I followed him. I was very frightened. So long as the stairs ran on the inside of the tower I got on well enough, but after 150 steps I felt the wind in my face, and we got to the place where the stairs were on the outside. The steps grew narrower and narrower and seemed to climb up to the sky.

"I shall never do it! " I cried.

"What! Are you afraid? Come on! " answered the professor.

I was forced to obey. I felt the tower move with the strong wind. I felt unsteady. I could not walk any longer. I had to creep up on my hands and knees. I shut my eyes. I felt sick.

At last I got to the top.

"Look down," said my uncle, "and look well. We must take lessons in looking down from heights."

I opened my eyes. I saw the houses looking small and flat. Above my head the clouds were moving, but to me it seemed as if they were standing still, while the tower and the town and the whole world were flying. In the distance, on one side was the green country and on the other the blue sea. Far away was the coast of Sweden.

My uncle made me stand up and look down. My first lesson lasted an hour, and when at last I was allowed to go down, and my feet touched the stones of the street, I felt like a man who has lost the use of his legs.

"We will begin again, tomorrow," said my uncle.

And so we did. For five days, one after another, we took this lesson, and in spite of myself I learnt how to look down without being frightened and without losing my sense of balance.

At last came the day for us to start. Our good friend, Professor Thomson, gave us letters to the governor of Iceland and to the chief citizen of Reykjavik, for which my uncle thanked him by a violent handshake.

On the 2nd at six o'clock in the morning our luggage was carried on the *Valkyrie*, and the captain received us.

"How is the wind?" asked my uncle.

"Excellent!" answered Captain Byarne. "From the southeast."

A few minutes later the ship was sailing through the narrow seas. An hour afterwards Copenhagen seemed to sink below the waves, and the *Valkyrie* was passing Elsinore. In my state of excitement I almost expected to see Hamlet[1] walking up and down on the tower of the castle.

---

[1] *Hamlet*, the Prince of Denmark, is the subject of one of Shakespeare's great plays. He was driven mad at Elsinore.

"Hamlet! You great and famous madman!" I said to myself. "What do you think of our mad journey? You would probably like to come with us to the centre of the earth and find there the answer to your everlasting doubt!"

But nothing came into sight on those old walls. As a matter of fact the castle is younger than the Prince of Denmark. It is now used as the shipping station of the Sound, through which 15,000 ships of all countries pass every year.

Soon the castle of Elsinore could no longer be seen. The town of Helsingborg on the Swedish coast also passed from our sight, and the ship began to catch the winds of the Kattegat.

The *Valkyrie* was a good ship, but after all, a sailing ship has to depend upon the wind.

"When shall we reach Reykjavik?" my uncle asked the captain.

"In about ten days' time," was the answer. "That is to

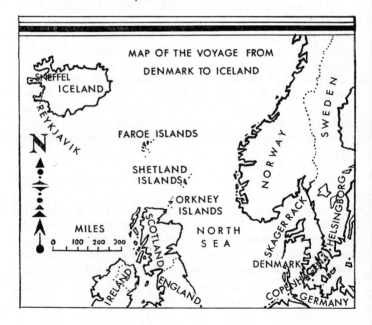

MAP OF THE VOYAGE FROM
DENMARK TO ICELAND

say if we do not get a north-west wind as we pass the Faroe Islands."

"But do you generally get there in good time?"

"Yes, Professor Lidenbrock. Make your mind easy; we shall get there soon enough."

Towards evening the ship passed the Skagen, the most northern point of Denmark, and during the night we passed through the Skager Rack, went along the southern coast of Norway and so out into the North Sea.

Two days later the coast of Scotland came in sight, and we then made our way towards the Faroe Islands, passing between the Orkney and Shetland Islands.

The waves of the Atlantic were soon breaking against our ship, and we had some difficulty with the wind. On the 8th we came in sight of the Faroe Islands, and from that time went straight towards Cape Portland, on the south coast of Iceland.

Nothing particular happened while we were on our way. I was quite well, but my uncle, who was sick the whole time, passed his time lying down. You may well imagine how angry and ashamed he was. I could not feel very sorry for him.

On the 11th Cape Portland came into sight. The Cape is simply a low hill with very steep sides, standing alone on the shore.

The *Valkyrie* kept a good way out from the coast and made its way towards the west. An immense rock was seen with large holes in it, through which the waves ran violently. After this we went right round Cape Reykyaness, which is the most western point of Iceland.

Because of the rough sea my uncle was not able to come up to admire the broken, rocky coast against which the waves were beating with great force.

Forty-eight hours later, after a rather severe storm, we saw the light of Cape Skagen, whose dangerous rocks run out below the waves for a long distance.

Three hours afterwards the *Valkyrie* came to a stop near the town of Reykjavik.

The professor came up at last, with a white face and

feeling very tired. But he was as happy and excited as ever, and his eyes were shining with satisfaction.

The people of the town stood in a group on the shore, particularly interested because the ship had brought them many things of which they were in need.

My uncle, of course, was in a great hurry to leave the ship, but before doing so he pulled me to the side and, pointing to the north of the bay, showed me a great mountain with two high points covered by everlasting snow.

" Sneffel! Sneffel! " he cried.

Then telling me again to say nothing about the business that had brought us to the island, he took his place in the boat that was waiting for us. I followed, and a few minutes later our feet touched the shore of Iceland.

The next moment a fine-looking man came up. He was the governor of Iceland—Baron Trampe himself. The professor soon found out who he was and gave him the letters from Copenhagen. Then followed a short talk in Danish, of which, of course, I did not understand a word. As a result of this talk the governor promised my uncle that he would do all that he could to help.

From the chief citizen, Mr Finsen, my uncle received a most kind welcome.

There was another man, too, whom we met. This was Mr Fridriksson, the teacher of science at the school of Reykjavik. He spoke only Icelandic and Latin. It was in Latin that he spoke to us when he offered us his services. I felt at home with him at once, because, as a matter of fact, he was the only person with whom I could talk during the whole of my stay in Iceland.

There were only three rooms in his house, and two of these he kindly offered to us. And in these two rooms we settled down. The large amount of luggage that we brought with us was a matter that rather surprised the good people of Reykjavik.

" Come now, Axel," said my uncle, " we are making good progress. The worst part of the business is over."

" What do you mean? " I cried.

" Why, all we have to do now is to go down."

"Oh, if you think of it in that way, you are right; but we have to get up as well as to get down."

"Oh, that does not trouble me at all. Come, there is no time to waste. I am going to the library. Perhaps there is some writing of Saknussemm's to be found there, and if so I very much want to see it."

"And while you are there I will go and see the town. Won't you do that too? "

"No, I don't care about that at all. The interesting part of Iceland is not what is on top but what is below."

I went out and walked about. It would have been difficult to lose one's way in Reykjavik, as there are only two streets in it, so there was no need for me to ask my way—which anyhow I should not have been able to do.

The town lies between two hills on ground that is rather flat and wet. On one side a bed of lava slopes down to the sea. On the other is the wide Bay of Faxa. In this bay I could see the *Valkyrie*. The longer of the two streets runs in the same direction as the shore. It is in the wooden houses of this street that the business men live. The other street, more to the west, runs down to a little lake.

I soon made my way through these grey, unhappy-looking streets, seeing here and there a little short, brown grass, or sometimes a poor-looking garden.

Not far off, on a hill, I saw the school where, as I was told afterwards, Danish, English and French are taught; three languages of which, I am ashamed to say, I did not know one word.

In three hours I had explored the town and some of the country round it. It looked an unhappy place. No trees, hardly any grass; everywhere volcanic rocks.

During my walk I met few people. In coming back through the business street I saw most of the people of the town drying and packing fish. The men looked well-built but heavy, rather like Germans; with light-coloured hair. I felt sorry for them; they seemed so far away from the world, living in this land of ice. Sometimes they gave a sort of

sudden laugh, but they never smiled. The women had pleasant faces, but they did not look happy.

When I went back to the house after my walk, I found my
uncle there with Mr Fridriksson.

5

PREPARATIONS

DINNER was ready, and as Professor Lidenbrock had eaten
little or nothing for some days past, you may imagine how
much he ate. I thought he would never finish eating. The
dinner was more Danish than Icelandic, but Mr Fridriksson
was more Icelandic than Danish. It was clear that he looked
upon the house more as ours than as his while we stayed
with him.

The talk was chiefly in the language of the country,
although sometimes my uncle used a little German, and
Mr Fridriksson a little Latin, so that I could understand
something of what was said. They were talking about
scientific subjects—particularly geology, but Professor Lidenbrock was very careful about what he said, and kept warning
me by a look to be careful not to say a word about our plans.

Almost the first question asked by Mr Fridriksson was
whether my uncle had found any interesting books at the
library.

"The library!" said my uncle. "Why, I only saw a few
uninteresting books. How is it possible to have such a poor
library!"

"And yet," said Mr Fridriksson, "we have 8,000 books
many of them very valuable and rare, and besides the works
in the old Icelandic language we have all the new books
that Copenhagen can send us."

"And where are those 8,000 books?"

"They are all over the country. In this old island of ours
we like studying. You will not find anybody here who can-

not read, and whose does not read. We think that it is better for books to be worn out by use than for us to keep them in a room where nobody can get at them. These books, then, are passed freely from one to another; they are read and read again, and often only come back here after they have been away for a year or two."

"And so," said my uncle, not too well pleased, " strangers ____"

"Strangers," said Mr Fridriksson, "have their own libraries at home, and our first business it to help our own people to study. I say again that the love of study is in the Icelandic blood. And now, if you will tell me what were the books you expected to find, I may perhaps be able to tell you something about them."

I looked at my uncle. He had now to answer, for this was a matter that was important for his plan. After thinking for a few moments he said:

" Mr Fridriksson, I want to know whether there are any writings of Arne Saknussemm among the old papers."

" Arne Saknussemm! " answered the teacher. " You mean a learned man who lived three hundred years ago, who was a great man of science, and a great traveller."

" Yes."

" One of the greatest men of this island."

" Exactly."

" A famous man in all countries."

" That's the man."

" As brave as he was learned."

" Ah, I see you know all about him."

My uncle smiled at the way in which Mr Fridriksson spoke of the man he admired so much, and he listened with great attention to every word.

" Well," he said at last, " and what about his books? "

" Ah! his books; we haven't any of them."

" What! Not in Iceland? "

" They are to be found neither in Iceland nor anywhere else."

" And why? "

" Because Arne Saknussemm was thought to be an enemy of the Church, and so all his books were burnt at Copenhagen."

"Very good! Splendid! " cried my uncle, to the great surprise of the teacher.

" What? " he cried.

" Yes," my uncle went on. " I see it all, now; everything is clear, and I can understand how it was that Saknussemm was forced to hide his secret in a cryptogram."

" What secret? " asked Mr Fridriksson, sharply.

" A secret that—that—which——"

" Is it some secret paper that you have found? "

" No, no; I was only supposing."

" Oh, I see," said Mr Fridriksson, and then, seeing how uncomfortable my uncle looked, was kind enough to talk about something else. " I hope," he said, " that you will not leave the island without making a study of its geology."

" Certainly not; but I am afraid I have come too late to make any new discovery. Scientific men must have visited this island more than once."

" Yes, Mr Lidenbrock. There have been many. But, believe me, there is plenty to do yet."

" Do you think so? " said my uncle, trying to look as if he were not interested.

" I do. How many mountains and volcanoes there are about which little or nothing is known! Take, for example, that mountain that you see over there. That is Sneffel."

" Ah, indeed! " answered my uncle. " That is Sneffel? "

" Yes; one of the most interesting volcanoes, and it is very few people who have ever been down its crater."

" Is it no longer active? "

" Yes, it has not been active for the last five hundred years."

My uncle, I am sure, wanted to jump into the air with excitement, but made a great effort to hide his feelings.

" Well then," he said, " I should like to begin by going to study that crater. What did you say the name of the mountain was? "

This part of the talk was in Latin. I understood every word of it. I could hardly stop myself laughing to see my uncle trying to hide his satisfaction. He did not know what to do so as not to show how pleased he was.

"Yes," he said. "What you have told me has made me decide to go up Sneffel and perhaps even study its crater."

"I am very sorry," said Mr Fridriksson, "that I shall not be able to come with you. I have my work, you see, and I cannot leave it."

"Oh, no, no, no," answered my uncle, quickly, "we should not like to trouble you, Mr Fridriksson. I thank you very much. You would have been very useful to us, I am sure, but your work, of course——"

It pleases me to think that Mr Fridriksson, with his simple trusting nature, did not notice my uncle's efforts to hide his secret.

"Your plan of beginning with Sneffel is a good one," he said. "You will find very interesting things there. But now, tell me, how do you intend to get there?"

"By sea. The quickest way will be to go across the bay."

"No doubt; but it is impossible to do it."

"Why?"

"Because at present there are no boats in Reykjavik. All our boats are on the other side of the island, where the men are fishing."

"What a pity!"

"You'll have to go by land—keeping along the shore. It's a longer way, but more interesting."

"Very well, then. I must find a guide."

"I know one who would suit you, I think."

"A good man, who can be trusted?"

"Yes, he lives not far from here. He is a very clever fellow, and I am sure he will please you. He speaks Danish perfectly."

"And when can I see him?"

"Tomorrow, if you like."

"Why not today?"

"Because he won't be here till tomorrow."

"Well, it must be tomorrow, then," said my uncle.

This important talk came to an end a little later, when my uncle thanked the Icelandic teacher sincerely for his great kindness. My uncle had learnt very much during the dinner. He had learnt the history of Saknussemm, the reason for the cryptogram, that Mr Fridriksson could not come with us, and that the next day a guide would be ready to do all we might want him to do.

In the evening I went for a short walk along the shore, and came back early. I then went to my room and was soon asleep in my big bed.

When I woke up in the morning I heard my uncle talking in the next room. I got up at once and made haste to join him.

He was talking Danish to a very tall man with a strong well-built body. This man had a very large head and a pleasant, simple-looking face. He looked as if he must be clever with his head and his hands. His eyes were light blue, and long hair, nearly red in colour, fell to his shoulders. His movements were easy and natural, although he never moved his hands or arms when he spoke. Everything about him showed calmness. He looked as if he could not be worried by anything or surprised at anything.

I could see all this by the way the Icelander listened to the stream of words that burst from my uncle's mouth. He stood absolutely still while my uncle was throwing his arms about. If he wanted to say yes, he moved his head up and down; if he wanted to say no, he turned it from left to right. But he moved his head so slowly and calmly that his long hair hardly moved.

His name was Hans Byelke. Mr Fridriksson had brought him to us. This was our future guide. I could not imagine anyone more different, in his appearance or in his behaviour, from my uncle.

They soon understood each other. Neither of them cared much about the matter of payment; one was ready to take what was offered, the other was ready to give what was asked. It was a very simple business arrangement.

The result of the agreement was that Hans would take us

to the village of Stapi on the southern side of, and at the foot of, Sneffel. The distance by land was only about twenty-two miles, a two days' journey, my uncle decided. But when he found that in a Danish mile there are 24,000 feet he was forced to change his plans and, as the roads were very bad, to allow seven or eight days.

We got four horses, two to carry my uncle and myself, and two for our luggage. Hans would walk—as he always did. He knew this part of the coast perfectly, and promised to take us the shortest way.

His arrangement with my uncle was not to come to an end at Stapi. He would stay in his service during the whole time of our journey. But our guide made a condition that his money should be paid to him regularly every Saturday evening.

We meant to start on the 16th of June. My uncle wished to give Hans some of his money at once, but the man refused by saying:

"*Efter.*"

"After," said my uncle to me.

"He is a good fellow," said the professor, as Hans left us, "but he has no idea of the wonderful thing he is going to do in the future."

"He will go with us, then, into——"

"Yes, Axel, into the centre of the earth."

We had still forty-eight hours before starting, but we had to spend them all in getting ready. We had to find the best way to pack everything, the instruments on this side, the guns on the other, the tools in this package, the food in the other; in all four groups.

Among the instruments were:

1. A thermometer[1] measuring temperature to 150 degrees, that seemed to me too much or too little. Too much if the heat of the air rose to that point, in which case we should be cooked; not enough if we had to measure the heat of boiling water or other liquids.

[1] see page 47.

2. A special barometer[1] made to show air-pressures greater than those found on the surface of the earth or higher. An ordinary barometer would not have been suitable, for as we went down into the earth the pressure of the air would become greater and greater.

3. A chronometer[1] measuring the exact time according to the position of Hamburg.

4. Two compasses.[1]

5. Two lamps which made their own electric light, these being safe, easy to carry and weighing little.

Then we had two guns. Why we took them I do not know. There were no enemies and no wild animals to fear, I supposed.

Among the tools were two picks,[1] a ladder of silk rope, three sticks with iron points, an axe, a hammer, and long ropes. All these made a big and heavy package, because the ladder was three hundred feet long.

Then there was the food. This was chiefly in the form of powders and pressed meat. It did not take up much room, but there was enough for six months. We took water-bottles but no water with us, for my uncle was trusting to fill the bottles from the underground springs that we should find.

This was not all. We had medicines, and all sorts of instruments used by doctors, things that would be useful in case of accidents, wounds and broken bones.

I cannot here describe all the other things we took with us. It is enough for me to say that my uncle seemed to have forgotten nothing. He even took money with him! And quite a large amount, too. Did he expect to find shops at the centre of the earth?

"There is no reason," said my uncle, "why, with all the things we are taking with us, we should not go far."

We passed the 14th of June arranging all our things. In the evening we had dinner with the governor, the chief citizen, and others. Mr Fridriksson, I am sorry to say, was not with us. I heard later that he and the governor had

[1] see page 47.

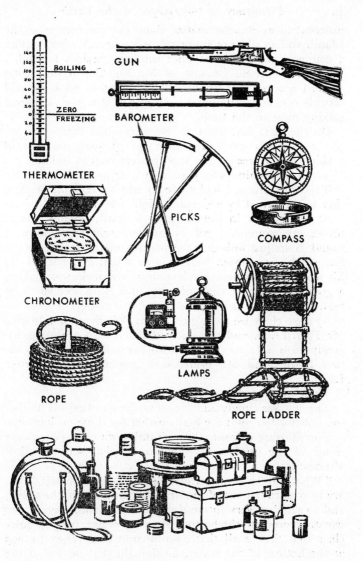

THERMOMETER

GUN

BAROMETER

PICKS

COMPASS

CHRONOMETER

LAMPS

ROPE

ROPE LADDER

different ideas on some matter about the government of the island, and so did not speak to each other. As this is quite a common happening in other countries besides Iceland, I was not surprised. Because of Mr Fridriksson not being there, I was not able to understand a word of what was said on this occasion. All that I noticed was that my uncle was talking most of the time.

On the next day, the 15th, we were quite ready to start. Mr Fridriksson gave my uncle the greatest pleasure in making him a present of a most perfect map of Iceland.

The last evening was passed in a serious talk with Mr Fridriksson, whom I had come to admire very much. And this was followed by a sleepless night for me.

At five o'clock in the morning I heard the four horses under my window. I got up at once and went down. I found Hans just finishing the packing of the things on the horses, almost without moving, one might say, but he did his work with uncommon cleverness. My uncle was making a great noise rather than helping, and Hans seemed to be taking no notice at all of what he was saying.

By six o'clock we were quite ready. We shook hands with Mr Fridriksson, and my uncle thanked him again for his goodness to us. I, too, thanked him as well as I could in my best Latin. And Mr Fridriksson answered me in better Latin.

Then we started.

The sky was cloudy and grey, but the weather was neither too hot nor too cold; the best weather for those on journeys.

The pleasure of going through unknown country took my mind off the unpleasant thoughts of what was to follow afterwards.

"What danger is there, after all?" I asked myself. "We are to go through one of the strangest countries in the world, and to climb a very interesting mountain and, even at the worst, go down to the bottom of an old crater, for it is quite clear that that is all that Saknussemm did. When he was at the bottom of the crater, he thought that he was at the centre of the earth. As to there being any real passage to the real centre of the earth, that is just imagination, and nothing more. It is an impossibility, so I shall get all the pleasure I can out of the business, and not trouble about the rest."

By the time that I had come to this decision, we had left Reykjavik far behind.

Hans was walking in front of us, and walking fast. The two horses with the luggage followed him. My uncle and I came along behind.

After leaving Reykjavik, Hans kept along the coast. We went through fields that tried their best to look green, and yet never succeeded in looking anything except yellow. We saw distant mountains, covered with snow. The tops of some of the mountains went up through the clouds, and looked like islands in the sky.

Our road was not a straight one. Sometimes the rocky hills ran out into the sea and the road went round them. But there was always room to pass. Our horses always knew the best way. They moved so well and so quickly that my uncle could not be impatient with them. I smiled to see such a big man on such a small horse. His long legs nearly touched the ground.

" Good horse! " he said. " You will see, Axel, that there is no better animal than an Icelandic horse. Nothing stops him; neither the snow, nor storms, nor bad roads. He is brave and goes on all the time. He never makes a wrong step. If we have to cross a river—and it is certain that we shall have to cross them—you will see him go into the water as if water or land were the same thing to him. But we must not be rough with him; we must let him go his own way, and we shall travel thirty miles a day."

" Yes, that is all right for us, but what about our guide? "

" Oh, he will be all right, too. Men like him get over the ground without noticing it. He will never get tired and if he does get tired, he can have my horse. If he can walk, I can walk too."

We were making good progress. The country looked very lonely. It was flat and covered with stones. In places we could see a poor-looking house built of wood and stone.

6

SNEFFEL

Two hours after leaving Reykjavik we reached a small village called Gufunus. It was not interesting at all.

Hans stopped there for half an hour. He had his breakfast with us, and said "yes" or "no" to all my uncle's questions, except when he was asked where we were to pass the night. He answered:

"Gardar."

I looked at the map to see where Gardar was, and found a little town of that name by the side of a river four (Danish) miles from Reykjavik. I showed it to my uncle.

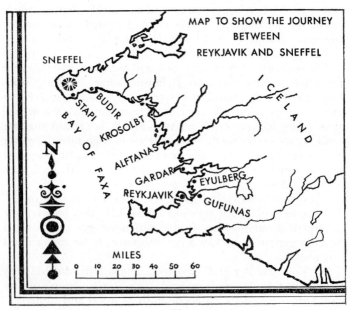

" Only four miles! " he said. " Four miles out of twenty-two! That's not bad."

He began talking to the guide about it, but he took no notice of what my uncle was saying, and walked on again. So we had to follow him.

Three hours later we passed through a village called Eyulberg. If there had been a clock there it would have shown us that it was twelve o'clock, but Icelandic churches are not rich enough to have clocks.

Here we gave our horses something to eat. After that we followed a narrow road between the hills and the sea.

At four o'clock we had gone four miles, which means twenty English miles. Here we were stopped by an arm of the sea going far into the land.

It was half a mile wide. The waves were breaking noisily over the sharp rocks. On each side of it there were walls of rock going up 2,000 feet. Our horses might be good horses, but I did not see how they were going to get across.

" If they are really as clever as people say," I thought to myself, " they will not try to cross it."

But my uncle would not wait. He went right on to the edge of the water. His horse stopped. My uncle tried to make the horse go on. The horse would not go on. My uncle said " yes "; the horse said " no ". My uncle got angry and struck the horse. The horse tried to throw my uncle off. At last the little horse bent his knees and walked out from between the legs of the professor, leaving him standing on the ground.

My uncle was surprised and angry.

Then Hans touched him and said, " *Farja.*"

" What? A boat? "

" *Der!* " answered Hans, pointing to a boat.

" Yes, there," I said, " I see a boat over there."

" Why didn't you say so before, then? Well, let's go and get it."

" *Tidvatten,*" said the guide.

" What is he saying? " I asked.

" The tide," said my uncle.

" He means that we must wait for the tide."

We had to wait until six o'clock in the evening, and then my uncle, myself, the guide and the two boatmen took our places in the boat.

It took us more than an hour to get over, but we got over safely.

Half an hour afterwards, we got to the village of Gardar.

It should have been quite dark, because it was night, but in Iceland during the months of June and July the sun is in the sky day and night. But it was very cold, and I was very hungry.

Hans soon found a place in which we could pass the night. It was only a rough hut, but what did that matter? It was warm, there was plenty of room for us, and there was enough food for all.

The master of the house came out to meet us, and asked us to follow him. We did so. We went into a long, dark, narrow passage. All the rooms opened into this passage. There were four of them: the kitchen, the workroom, the sleeping-room for the family, and, best of all, a visitors' room. We were taken to this room at once. For beds there were two box-like arrangements, painted red and filled with dry grass. I did not expect such comfort. The only thing I did not like was the unpleasant smell of dried fish. When we had taken off our travelling clothes we heard the voice of the master of the house inviting us into the kitchen, the only room in which there was a fire, even in the coldest weather.

My uncle went first, and I followed him.

The fire-place of the kitchen was on the ground in the middle of the room, and a hole at the top of the room above it let out the smoke. The kitchen was at the same time the dining-room.

When we went in, we received a warm welcome from the husband and wife. Each said the word *sallvertu*, which means " be happy ", after which they laid their right hands on their hearts, and bowed.

This Icelandic woman, let me say, was the mother of nineteen children, big and little, running around in the room.

At every moment some little head and rather unhappy face would look out of the clouds of smoke that filled the room.

My uncle and I soon had three or four of these children sitting on our shoulders and our knees. Those who could speak said " *sallvertu* ", and those who could not, made loud cries—which perhaps meant the same thing.

After a short time Hans came in. He had been outside to see that the horses had food, and this he did by letting them out in the fields to find what food they could.

" *Sallvertu!* " said Hans, and shook hands with the husband and wife and each of the nineteen children.

When this was done, we sat down to table, twenty-four in number, so there was not much room. Most of us had at least two children on our knees.

When the meal was over the children went out of the room and the rest of us sat round the fire talking. Of course I was not able to understand a word of what was said.

Later we got ready for the night's sleep. The good woman offered to undress us—it is usual in Iceland for the lady of the house to undress visitors—and after we had refused politely, she left us, and I was at last able to get to my bed of grass.

At five o'clock the next morning we said good-bye to these good people. It was only with difficulty that we made them accept the money we offered for our room and meal.

We started.

About a hundred steps from Gardar the ground began to look different. It became soft and wet, and it was more difficult for us to travel. On our right the mountains grew higher and higher and went on and on into the far distance. Often we came to streams which we had to cross carefully to prevent our luggage from getting wet.

As we went on, the country grew more and more lonely. There was no more grass and there were no longer any trees; there were no animals, except a few horses trying to find food. Sometimes we could see some large bird flying away towards the south.

Before long we had to cross several unimportant rivers

and then a wide arm of the sea. The tide being low just then, we got over easily and reached the village of Alftanas, about one mile beyond.

In the evening, having crossed two more rivers, we had to pass the night in an empty hut.

Nothing unusual happened the next day. There was still the same soft watery ground, the same loneliness, and the same greyness. By the evening we had finished half our journey, and spent the night at Krosolbt.

On the 19th of June we walked for about a mile over a bed of lava. Here the rocks stood up in the strangest shapes, with sharp, rough edges, making it difficult for us to go forward. In some places steam shot up from the hot springs below the ground.

We went on steadily, now towards the west. In fact we had gone right round the great bay of Faxa, and the white tops of Sneffel stood up against the clouds less than five miles away. I began to feel very tired, but my uncle showed no sign of any weakness. I could only admire him. As for Hans, he thought of this journey as a pleasant walk.

On Saturday, 20th of June, at six o'clock in the evening we reached Budir, a village on the seashore. Here Hans said that it was time to receive his money, and my uncle paid him. The place was our guide's home, and it was his family —that is, his uncles and cousins—who received us. They were very kind to us, and I should have been glad to stay there a little, to rest myself after these five tiring days. But my uncle, who had no need of rest, wanted only one thing, and that was to go forward and stop as little as possible; and so the next morning we got on our horses again.

As the day went on we got nearer and nearer to the great mountain. The professor could not stop looking at it. I could sometimes hear him talking to himself: "Sneffel," he said. "Oh! great Sneffel! The gate that opens to the centre of the earth! Saknussemm! Arne Saknussemm! We are here!"

Our day's journey came to an end at Stapi, a village of about thirty huts built of lava. It lies along the side of a small arm of the sea.

The next day we got ready to go up the mountain. Our horses would be of no further use, and our luggage was to be carried by three Icelanders.

My uncle now told Hans that he meant to make an examination of the volcano, and go to the bottom of its crater, no matter how deep it might be.

Hans simply made a movement with his head, to show that he agreed. To go there or anywhere else was all the same to him. As for myself, now that I saw how near we were to the terrible dangers that lay before us, I was getting more and more frightened. But what was to be done? If I wished to refuse to go with my uncle or to stop him from going, the place for me to do so was Hamburg and not Sneffel. It was now too late.

One thought particularly made me feel anxious—a thought that would frighten anybody.

I said to myself, "We are going to the top of Sneffel. All

right. Very good. We are going to visit the crater. All right.
Very good. Others have done that, and they have come back
alive. But that is not all. If there should really be a passage
down into the earth, and if that terrible man, Saknussemm,
spoke the truth, we shall go and lose ourselves in the depths
under the volcano. But what is there to prove that Sneffel
is no longer active? Who knows whether it will not blow up?
The volcano has been asleep since the year 1229, but does
that prove that it will not wake up tomorrow? And if it
does wake up, what will happen to us?"

This was worth thinking about, and I did think about it.
I could not sleep without dreaming of exploding volcanoes,
and I must say that I did not like the idea of being shot up
to the sky by a bursting mountain.

At last I felt that I must speak to my uncle on the subject.
But I must speak to him not as if I were afraid of anything,
but as if I were trying to learn more about the nature of the
inside of the earth.

I went to him and told him about what I had been
thinking.

"How do we know, uncle," I asked, "whether an old
volcano will not suddenly become active again?"

I stopped and waited for the burst of anger that I
expected.

But all he said was:

"I have been thinking about it."

What could he mean? Was he really going to listen to the
voice of reason? Was it possible that he might not go on
with his plan after all? It could not be true.

After a few minutes, during which time I did not dare to
say anything, he said again:

"I was thinking of it. Ever since we reached Stapi, I have
been asking myself the same important question, for after
all we must not do anything unwise."

"No," I said. "You are quite right."

"For about a hundred years Sneffel has not spoken, but
he may yet speak. At the same time there is this that we
know: volcanoes never blow up without other things hap-

pening for some time before; they always give warning. So I have been asking questions of the people who live about here. I have examined the ground, and I am now able to say that there will be no explosion."

I was surprised at what he said, and could make no answer.

" Don't you believe me? " my uncle went on. " Well, come with me."

I went with him. The professor made his way through a passage in the wall of rock. Soon we were in the open country —if you can use the word " country " for a lonely stretch of rocks and stone.

In various places I could see little bursts of steam going up into the air. It seemed to me that these were a fairly strong proof of what I was afraid of. But my uncle went on to say:

" You see all this steam, Axel? Well, it shows that there is nothing to be afraid of."

" What do you mean? "

" Remember this," the professor went on; " when the time for a volcano to blow up is near, this steam comes out with greater and greater force, but during the explosion no more steam comes out at all. And the steam escapes by way of the crater, instead of through these holes in the ground. Now, as these bursts of steam are coming out as usual, and with no more force than usual, and also as a heavy dead calm has not taken the place of wind and rain, you may be quite sure that there will be no volcanic action."

" But——"

" Enough! When science has spoken, it is not for us to say anything."

I was very disappointed. My uncle had won, as usual. But there was still one hope; and this was that when we got to the bottom of the crater we should find no passage, in spite of what Saknussemm had written.

I passed a very bad night, dreaming that I was in the middle of a volcano down deep in the earth, and that I was then shot up to the sky.

The next day, the 22nd of June, Hans was ready waiting

C

for us, with his companions carrying the food, the tools and the instruments. My uncle and I carried the iron-pointed sticks. Hans, like a wise man, had added to our luggage a big bottle filled with water. This would be enough to last us for a week.

At nine o'clock we left Stapi, and started the long climb.

Sneffel is 5,000 feet high. From our starting-point we could not see its two high points, but only the sides of the mountain and the snow with which its top was covered.

We walked one behind the other, Hans going first, so it was impossible to talk.

In spite of my anxiety and fears, I was interested to notice the strange rocks of this part of the world, and I thought of the whole geological history of Iceland.

As we know, in past times, millions of years ago, most of what is now dry land was covered by the sea. As time went on, little by little, the land was gradually pushed up and came to form the world as it is today. It is clear that Iceland came up out of the sea not so very long ago—perhaps even not more than twenty or thirty million years ago. Perhaps it is still slowly pushing its way little by little up out of the sea. If this is so, something must be pushing from below. Is it the heat deep down in the earth? If so, the ideas of Humphry Davy and my uncle, and the writing of Saknussemm must be all wrong.

Everything that I noticed during our journey seemed to show that there must be an immense degree of heat far down below. And the farther down that one went, the heat must be greater and greater. And yet my uncle was expecting to get to the centre of the earth! Madness! Fortunately, it would be impossible. Even my uncle would turn back long before we got to the point where our road would pass through boiling and melting rocks!

These thoughts made me feel happier.

The road became more and more difficult. It was going up more and more steeply. Hans walked along easily, as if the ground were quite flat. At times, when he turned to the left or the right beyond some great rock, we could not see him. Often, too, he picked up some pieces of rock and arranged them in such a way that they would help us to find our way back. This was a good idea of his, although, as we shall see later, it was needless.

After three hours of tiring walking, we were only, after all, at the foot of the mountain. There Hans said that we had better stop for a short time so that we could have something to eat. My uncle was so anxious to get on that he ate twice as fast as the rest of us. But we had stopped not only for breakfast, but for a rest, and Hans did not call on us to start until after an hour had passed. The three Icelanders said as little as Hans—or less.

Now the real work began. The top of the mountain seemed very near, but how many hours it took us to get there! And what work! The stones and rocks were all loose, and as we walked they slipped under our feet and went rolling down the hill-side.

The mountain grew steeper and steeper; it was impossible to climb up straight; we had to go sideways—and this was not easy. We helped each other with our sticks.

I must say that my uncle kept as close to me as possible. He helped me many times with his arm. He must have been very good at mountain climbing, for he never fell once. In spite of the fact that the Icelanders had so much to carry, they climbed easily and without stopping.

It seemed almost impossible that we should ever get to the top.

At seven o'clock in the evening we had gone up 2,000 feet of the mountain. We were already higher than the bottom of the crater. The sea was 3,200 feet below us. We were now in the snow. It was terribly cold. The wind blew violently. I was almost tired out. The professor saw how tired I was, and, in spite of his impatience, he decided to stop. He told Hans to stop, but Hans shook his head, and said:

" *Ofvanfor.*"

" He means that we must go higher, it seems," said my uncle, and asked the reason.

" *Mistour,*" answered our guide.

"*Ja, mistour,*" said one of the Icelanders, in a voice that showed us that he was frightened of something.

"What does he mean?" I asked.

"Look!" answered my uncle.

I looked down below. An immense quantity of stones, sand and volcanic dust was flying round and round up into the air. The wind was driving it towards this side of the mountain on which it threw a great shadow. It was coming straight towards us, and if we were caught in it we should be carried up into the air with it. It was what is called in Icelandic a *mistour*.

"*Hastigt, hastigt!*" cried our guide.

Although I did not understand Danish, I knew he meant that we were to make haste and follow him. He began to go round towards the other side of the mountain. Before long all this stony stuff fell with a *crash* on the mountain. The ground on which we were standing shook. Fortunately we had got round to the other side, and were safe. But if our guide had not warned us, our bodies would have been thrown into the air, torn to pieces, and carried away by the wind.

Hans did not think it wise to pass the night on the side of the mountain, so we had to go on climbing, and it took us five hours before we got to the top. I was almost dead with cold and hunger. The air was so thin that it was difficult to breathe. It was eleven o'clock at night when we found ourselves on the top, and before I went down into the crater with the others, I had time to see the midnight sun at its lowest point shining weakly on the island that lay at my feet.

We soon had our meal and we arranged ourselves as well as we could. Our bed was hard; the air was cold—and this is not surprising, as we were 5,000 feet above the sea. But in spite of everything I slept well. In fact it was the best sleep that I had had for a long time. I did not even dream.

7

GOING DOWN

WHEN we woke up the next morning, we felt very cold. The sun was shining when I got up from my stony bed and went out to see the beautiful sight.

I was on the top of one of the two high points—the one on the south. I could see almost the whole of the island. It looked like a map spread out below me.

The professor and Hans joined me.

My uncle turned to the west and pointed to something far away that looked like smoke or steam resting on the top of the sea, and said:

" That's Greenland."

" Greenland? " I cried.

" Yes, we are only about a hundred miles away from it. You didn't know, Axel, did you, that a part of America could be seen from a part of Europe? "

Then my uncle went on:

" We are on the top of Sneffel, and here are two high points, one to the south and the other to the north. Hans will tell us what the Icelanders call the one that we are on now." He turned to Hans and asked him the question, and Hans answered:

" Scartaris."

My uncle gave me a look of immense satisfaction, and said:

" Then let us start for the crater! "

The crater of Sneffel was about three miles wide. It seemed to be about 2,000 feet deep. Imagine what it must look like when full of fire and burning rock! The bottom of the crater could not be more than 500 feet round, so it was quite easy to walk down. Hans took his place at the head of our group. I followed.

In some places we found deep ice. At these places Hans walked very carefully, and struck the ground with his stick at every step to make sure that it was safe to pass. Where it seemed more dangerous we fastened ourselves together with a long rope, so that if any one of us fell, he would be held up by the others. This was a wise arrangement, but all the same there was some danger.

Although it was difficult to go down, and the journey was a new one for our guide, there was no accident.

At twelve o'clock we got to the bottom. I looked up and saw the mouth of the crater against the sky. It was perfectly round. Just on the edge of it I could see the sunny top of Scartaris.

At the bottom of the crater were three holes, really the tops of chimneys out of which the central fire of Sneffel had shot its fire and smoke. Each of these chimneys was about a hundred feet wide. It made me feel frightened to look at them. But Professor Lidenbrock quickly examined all three of them. He ran from one to the other in a most excited state, making the most violent movements, and talking to himself. Hans and his companions, sitting on the rocks, looked at him and wondered what he was doing and saying. They clearly thought him mad.

Suddenly my uncle gave a cry. I thought that he was falling into one of the holes. But no, there he was, with his arms and legs stretched out, standing in front of an immense rock in the centre of the crater. He stood there like a man so struck with wonder that he is not yet able to form any clear thoughts, but when clear thoughts came to him he was almost mad in his wild happiness.

" Axel! " he cried, at last, " Axel, Axel! Come here! "

I ran to him. Neither Hans nor his companions moved.

" Look! " said the professor.

If I was not happy, as he was, I was at least as surprised as he was, for on the face of this rock, in Runic letters, half eaten away by time, was the name, the terrible name:

" Arne Saknussemm! " cried my uncle. " Have you still any doubt? "

I did not answer. I could not answer. I went and sat down on a rock. This was too much for me. There was nothing more to be said. How long I sat there in a state of wonder and anxiety I cannot say. All I know is that when I looked up again only Hans and my uncle were with me in the crater. The Icelanders had gone and were on their way back to Stapi.

Hans was sleeping quietly at the foot of a rock, where he had made a sort of bed for himself. My uncle was walking up and down like a wild animal. I had no wish to get up, and no strength to get up. So I did as Hans did, and went to sleep. But while I slept I seemed to hear the noises of the mountain and feel it shaking.

In this way I passed the first night at the bottom of the crater.

The next day the sky was grey and dark, and my uncle was violently angry.

I understood why he was angry, and I began to hope.

This was why:

There were three roads possible, and only one had been followed by Saknussemm. According to him, there was only one way to know which was the right one. It was the one on which the shadow of Scartaris fell during the last days of June.

But as there was no sun, there was no shadow. Nothing could tell us which of the three roads was the road that we should take. It was now the 25th of June, and if the sky were cloudy for four more days, we could do nothing until the next year.

No wonder my uncle was violently angry!

The day passed, and no shadow came in sight. Hans never moved, although he must have wondered what we were waiting for—if, indeed, he could wonder at all. My uncle never spoke to me. He did nothing but keep his eyes fixed on the grey sky.

On the 26th there was still no shadow. Rain and snow

kept falling all day long. Hans made a hut with pieces of stone. I passed my time watching the thousands of streams that kept running down the sides of the crater.

I cannot describe my uncle's anger and impatience. And certainly it was enough to make a far more patient man angry.

The next day, again, was dull. No sun; no blue sky; no shadow. But on Sunday, the 28th of June, the last day but two of the month, with the change of moon came the change of weather. The sun sent its brightness down into the depths of the crater. Every hill, every rock, every stone was shining in the sunlight, and each threw its shadow on the ground. Among the others, we saw the shadow of Scartaris. It moved round with the sun. My uncle moved with it. At twelve o'clock it fell softly on the edge of the middle chimney.

" It's there! It's there! " cried the professor, adding in Danish: " Now let's get away to the centre of the earth! "

I looked at Hans.

" *Forut,*" was his quiet answer.

" Forward," said my uncle.

The real journey now began. Up to the present our journey had been more tiring than difficult, but from now there would be more and greater difficulties. I had not yet even looked down the bottomless chimney. The time had now come. I must now decide whether to go on with the others or stop. But I was ashamed to stop when Hans was ready to go on. Hans seemed afraid of nothing; he saw no danger; and how could I be less brave than he? If my uncle and I had been alone I should have started again telling him of my fears and showing him the foolishness and the impossibility of his plan. But how could I do this in front of our guide? So I said nothing. For a moment I thought of Gräuben, and her hopes of our success, and then I walked bravely to the edge of the middle chimney.

I have already said, I think, that it was a hundred feet wide, or three hundred feet round. Holding on to a rock I looked down the chimney. It was a terrible moment. My hair seemed to be standing up straight on my head. Everything seemed to be turning round. I think I was just going to fall when a strong hand held me back. It was Hans who was holding me. Evidently I had not taken enough lessons at Copenhagen in looking down.

The little that I had seen of this chimney had given me a good idea of what it was like. Although its walls went straight down, they were not smooth; in some places sharp rocks came out like steps. But there was nothing that our hands could catch hold of. A rope fastened to the edge would have been useful, but how could we unfasten it when we got to the end of the rope?

My uncle found a simple and clever way to deal with this difficulty. He took a piece of rope about the thickness of a finger and about 400 feet long. He let half of it go down first, and then put the middle of it around a rock that came out from the wall, and threw down the other half. Each of us could then go down by holding the two lines of rope. When we had gone down 200 feet nothing could be easier than to bring the rope down by pulling one end. Then we would begin again and again.

"Now," said my uncle, "let's see about the luggage. We will divide it into three parts, and each of us will fasten one part on his back. Of course, I mean only those things that are easily broken."

"Hans," he said, "will take the tools and a part of the food. You, Axel, will take the guns and another third of the food, and I will take the rest of the food and the scientific instruments."

"But who is to take the clothes," I asked, "and all those ropes?"

"They will take care of themselves."

"How?"

"You'll see."

He told Hans to make a big package of all the things that could not break, and throw them down.

I could hear the noise that the package made as it went through the air. The noise grew less and less, and at last I could hear nothing at all.

"That's all right," said my uncle. "Now let us go ourselves!"

I ask you, was it possible for anybody who was not quite mad to hear such words without being terribly frightened?

My uncle then fastened the instruments on his back, and Hans took the tools, and I took the guns. Hans went first, then my uncle, then myself. We said nothing. There was no noise except that of loose rocks falling down into the depths.

I let myself down, holding tight to the double rope in one hand, and supporting myself with my stick in the other. I had only one idea; I was afraid the rope would break, for it seemed too thin to carry the weight of three people. I used it as little as possible.

In about half an hour we found ourselves on a big, flat rock that stuck out from the wall of the chimney.

Hans pulled the rope by one end, and the other flew up. When it passed the rock on which it hung, it fell down, bringing with it a large number of loose stones.

I looked over the edge of our narrow rock, but still could see nothing below.

Then we arranged the rope again as before, and half an hour later we had gone another 200 feet.

I don't know whether the maddest geologist would have tried to study the nature of the rocks that he was climbing down. As for myself, I didn't trouble about it; I did not care what sort of rocks they were. But no doubt the professor was examining them closely, for he said to me:

"The farther I go the more certain I am that I am right. The arrangement of these rocks strongly supports the idea of Humphry Davy. I do not believe that the centre of the earth is at all hot. Anyhow, we shall soon see."

Always the same idea. I did not feel like saying anything that might make my uncle angry, and so, as I said nothing, my uncle supposed that I agreed with him.

We began going down again, but at the end of three

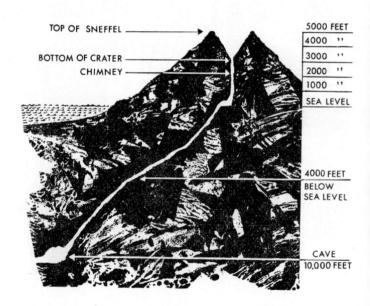

TOP OF SNEFFEL

BOTTOM OF CRATER

CHIMNEY

5000 FEET
4000 "
3000 "
2000 "
1000 "
SEA LEVEL

4000 FEET
BELOW
SEA LEVEL

CAVE
10,000 FEET

hours the bottom was not yet in sight. When I looked up I saw that the mouth of the chimney was getting smaller. It was gradually getting dark.

Still we went on; down, down. I had the idea that the loose stones were not falling so far, and that they made more noise. I had taken care to notice exactly how many times we had re-hung the rope so that I knew exactly how deep we were and how long the journey was taking us. It took us half an hour to go down the rope, and we had done so fourteen times. That meant that we had been climbing down for seven hours, and three hours and a half in addition for rest and meals. Ten hours and a half in all. We had started at one o'clock, so it must be eleven. As to the depth, fourteen times 200 feet gave a depth of 2,800 feet.

At this moment I heard the voice of Hans calling:

" Stop! "

I stopped at once, just in time to keep my feet from striking against my uncle's head.

" We are there! " he cried.

" Where? " I asked, stepping down by his side.

" At the bottom of the chimney."

" Then there is no way out? "

" Yes, there is a passage, I think, to the right. But we shall see tomorrow. It is time for a meal and then we must go to sleep."

We opened one of the bags, and took some food, and then we all three arranged ourselves as comfortably as we could on the stones.

As I lay on my back I saw a bright spot at the end of the chimney. It was a star.

Then I went to sleep.

8

"GIVE ME ONE MORE DAY"

A T eight o'clock the next morning we were woken up by the daylight that came 3,000 feet down to us. It was, of course, not a strong light, but just strong enough to let us see the things round us.

" Well, now, Axel, how do you like this? " asked my uncle, looking particularly pleased. " Did you ever pass a quieter night in the old house in Königstrasse? No street noises of any sort."

" Yes, certainly it is very quiet, but I don't like the quietness. It makes me feel rather frightened."

"Come, come," said my uncle. "If you are frightened now, how will you feel later? So far we have not gone one inch into the earth."

" What do you mean? "

" I mean that we are no lower than the sea. We have only come down the same distance that we went up when we climbed Sneffel."

" Are you sure of that? "

" Quite. Look at the barometer."

I found it showing twenty-nine inches.

" You see," said the professor, " we have only the ordinary pressure of the air."

" But as we go down, will not the pressure of the air get greater and greater, and make it more and more difficult for us to breathe? "

" We shall go down slowly, and gradually get used to the heavier air. It is better to have it too heavy than too light. But we are wasting time. Where is the package we threw down yesterday? "

Then I remembered that we had looked for it the night before and could not find it.

My uncle asked Hans about it. After looking round, Hans said:

"*Der huppe.*"

"Up there."

It was quite true. There was the bundle hanging to a rock a hundred feet above our heads. The Icelander quickly climbed up, and in a few minutes we had it again.

"Now," said my uncle, "let us have breakfast, and eat like men who are likely to have a long day's walk before them."

When we had finished our breakfast, my uncle took a note-book out of his pocket, looked at the different instruments and wrote down:

> *Monday, July 1st.*
>
> Chronometer: 8.17 in the morning.
> Barometer: 29.7.
> Thermometer: 6.
> Direction: East-South-East.

This last note meant the direction of the dark passage, and was given by the compass.

"Now, Axel," cried the professor in an excited voice, "we are really going down into the earth. This is the exact moment at which our journey begins."

Saying this, my uncle took with one hand the electric instrument that was hanging from his neck, and joined it to the electric lamp. It at once threw out a light bright enough for us to see everything clearly.

Hans was carrying the other lamp, which was lighted in the same way.

We each picked up our packages and fastened them to our backs. As for the big package of clothes and ropes, Hans was ready to roll it along in front of him.

"Forward," said my uncle, and we walked into the passage.

Just before I went into the dark passage I looked up and saw once more and for the last time in my life the sky of Iceland.

At the time of the last volcanic action, in the year 1229, the lava had forced this passage for itself, and the sides of it were covered with some shiny metallic stuff. It was a beautiful sight, and I could not help admiring it.

" It is splendid! " I cried. " Look at those colours, uncle! "

" Ah, you like it, Axel," answered my uncle. " You call it splendid, my boy; you will see many more things to admire, I hope. Let's walk on! "

My uncle should have said: " Let's slip on," for we were slipping more than walking. Indeed, the steepness of the road was our chief difficulty, and we had to take care not to fall. We were travelling towards the south-east, and the road went straight in this direction, turning neither to one side nor the other.

And yet it hardly got any warmer. Two hours after we started it was only four degrees warmer.

About eight o'clock in the evening my uncle told us to stop. Hans sat down at once. We hung our lamps on pieces of rock that stuck out from the sides of the passage. We were in a sort of cave.

You would think that there would be no movement of the air, but this was not the case. At times we could feel a wind blowing. Where did it come from? But I was too tired and too hungry to think much about it. Seven hours of going down a slippery road takes much of one's strength away. So I was very pleased when I heard the order to stop. Hans brought out the food and spread it on a flat rock. But there was one thing that made me feel anxious: we had used half the water that we had brought with us. My uncle had expected to find underground springs, but so far not one had appeared. I could not help calling his attention to this fact.

" Are you surprised at finding no springs? " he asked.

" Yes, I am, and what is more, I am feeling anxious; we have water enough only for five days."

" Don't let that give you any anxiety," he answered. " I am certain that we shall find water, and as much as we want."

" When? "

" As soon as we get out of the lava walls. How could

springs burst through such walls as these? Springs of water cannot make their way through solid lava."

" But perhaps this passage runs to a great depth. It seems to me that we have not gone very far down."

" What makes you think that? "

" Because the heat would be very much greater if we had gone a long way down."

" That would be right if your idea of central heat were right. But your idea is wrong, and Humphry Davy is right. Look at the thermometer; what does it say? "

" It says fifteen degrees, which is only nine more than when we started."

" Well, and what do you think that means? "

" I think it means this: According to all that we know of the subject, and all that we have read on the subject, the heat becomes greater by one degree for every hundred feet that we go down. But near an old volcano, where the rocks are very solid, the heat becomes greater by one degree for every 125 feet. Let us see what that makes."

" Yes, do so, my boy."

" Nothing is easier," I said, writing down the figures. " Nine times 125 feet makes 1,125 feet of depth."

" Exactly. But let me tell you this," said my uncle. " Instead of being only 1,125 feet down, we are 10,000 feet down. I have examined with the greatest care all through the day how far we have been going down, and there is no possible doubt about it. We have today gone down 10,000 feet."

What my uncle said was clearly true. He did not make mistakes in matters of this sort. We had already gone 6,000 feet below the greatest depth to which man had ever gone.

The temperature, then, which ought to have been eighty-one degrees, was hardly fifteen degrees.

It looked, then, as if my uncle and Humphry Davy were right, after all, and as if the centre of the earth were not such a hot place.

The next day, the 30th of June, at six o'clock in the morning we started off again. We still followed the passage through the lava. It was no longer so steep; it made its way downward gently, and we walked with greater ease. We went on until just after twelve o'clock. Hans, who had been walking in front of us, stopped.

"Ah!" cried my uncle, "then we have at last come to the end of the passage."

I looked round me. There were two new passages in front of us: one to the east, and the other to the west. Which one ought we to take? Here was a difficulty.

But my uncle did not wait. He pointed to the eastern passage and soon we were all three making our way along it.

It was a mistake. But it was many days before we discovered it.

This new passage was not at all a steep one. It went down very gently, too gently. I did not like it. I felt that there was something wrong, but did not like to tell my uncle what I felt.

By six o'clock in the evening, after a walk that was not at all tiring, we had gone six miles to the south, but were hardly a quarter of a mile deeper. We stopped. We had our supper. We said little, and went to sleep without thinking much.

We woke up the next morning feeling fresh and bright. We went on our way again. We followed the passage of lava as on the day before. It certainly no longer went down. It seemed to me to be going up. So much so, indeed, that by ten o'clock I felt tired and had to walk slowly.

"Come on, Axel! What's holding you back?" said the professor, impatiently.

"I must stop. I can't walk so fast," I answered.

"What? After walking only three hours on such an easy road?"

"Easy it may be, but it's very tiring."

"What? When it's all downhill?"

"Downhill? All uphill you mean! For the last half-hour

we've been walking upwards, and if we keep on like this it won't be long before we get back to Iceland."

The professor shook his head. He was not willing to listen to what I had to say. So we went on walking upwards. This was a good way, I thought, of getting back to Iceland, and later, to Copenhagen and Hamburg, but it was certainly not a good way to get to the centre of the earth.

By twelve o'clock I noticed a change in the appearance of the walls of the passage. Instead of lava I saw newer rocks arranged in regular beds. We were among the rocks of the Silurian age.

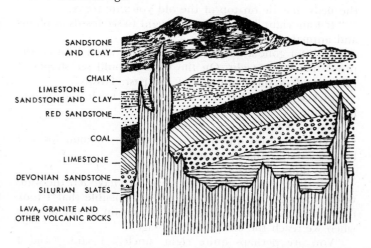

SANDSTONE AND CLAY—

CHALK—

LIMESTONE—
SANDSTONE AND CLAY—
RED SANDSTONE—

COAL—

LIMESTONE—

DEVONIAN SANDSTONE—
SILURIAN SLATES—

LAVA, GRANITE AND OTHER VOLCANIC ROCKS

I ought to have kept my thoughts to myself, but my interest in geology forced me to cry out in wonder at what I saw, and my uncle heard me.

"What's the matter with you?" he asked.

"Look," I answered, showing him the different sorts of rocks.

"Well?"

"We have left the lava below us and have come to the higher beds where there are fossils[1] of animals and plants."

[1] *Fossil:* stone-like remains of an animal or plant of the past.

" You think so? "

" But look! Examine the rocks for yourself."

I forced the professor to throw the light of the lamp on the sides of the passage. I expected him to cry out in surprise. But instead of doing that, he walked on without saying a word.

Had he understood or not? Was he unwilling to confess that he had been mistaken in choosing the passage to the east, or did he want to examine the passage to the end?

At the same time I wondered whether I was not making a mistake about the rocks. Were we really going through the beds that lie on top of the old volcanic rocks?

" If I am right," I thought, " I ought to see fossils of plants and animals. I will look."

I had not gone a hundred steps farther when I found the proof that I was right. On the walls I could see shapes of plants and of small animals of the past. Fossils!

I picked up a perfect one, ran up to my uncle and showed it to him.

" Look," I said.

" Well," he said quietly, " it is only a common fossil. I have many like that in Hamburg."

" But don't you see then, that——"

" Yes, I see exactly what you mean. We have left the solid volcanic rocks and lava below us. It is possible that I took the wrong path, but I shall only be certain of my mistake when we reach the end of this passage."

" You are perhaps quite right, uncle," I said, " and I should agree with you. But don't forget that there is a danger before us, a danger that is growing greater and greater at every moment."

" And what is that? "

" We have hardly any more water."

" Then we shall have to drink less," said my uncle.

And this indeed we were forced to do. Our water would not last three days longer. I saw that when supper-time came.

All the next day we walked on and on without saying a word. The road was not going up now, at least very little.

The rocks were still of the same sort. As we went on, it become more and more clear that we were not on the right road, but Professor Lidenbrock seemed not to notice it. He was expecting one of two things: either that we should find some new passage going straight down, or that the road would come to an end, and so stop us from going any farther. But evening came, and there was no change.

On Friday, after a night during which I was in great need of water, we again made our way along the narrow passage. After ten hours' walking, I noticed that the colour of the walls was changing. I saw shining black rocks. I happened to touch the wall with my hand, and when I took it away I saw that it was quite black. I looked more closely. It was coal!

" Look, uncle! Coal! "

" Yes, I know," said my uncle. " What does that matter? But it is now supper-time."

Hans got the meal ready. I hardly ate anything, and drank the little water that was given to me. After that we lay down for a rest. My two companions slept well, but I lay awake until the morning.

On Saturday, at six o'clock in the morning, we started off again. Twenty minutes later, we got to an immense cave a hundred feet wide and a hundred and fifty feet high. The walls were made of coal. We walked on through this cave until the evening, our road going neither up nor down. It was quite plain that in spite of the long distance we had walked, we were no nearer the centre of the earth. You may imagine the impatience of my uncle.

At six o'clock in the evening a wall appeared in front of us. There was no opening to the right or left, above or below. We had come to the end of the road.

" Well, that is good! " cried my uncle. " At least we know something; we know that this was the wrong road. Saknussemm never came this way at all. All we have to do now is to go back to the place where we saw the two roads."

" Yes," said I, " if we have enough strength."

" And why should we not have enough strength? "

" Because tomorrow we shall have no more water."

Just then Hans told my uncle that it was Saturday evening, and time for him to receive his money for the second week.

We decided to start as soon as possible. No time was to be wasted, because it would take us at least three days to get to the place where the two roads met.

Those were three terrible days. As I had said, the water came to an end on the evening of the first day. I cannot describe how much we suffered from thirst. At times I felt that I could walk no longer. More than once I fell. Then we had to stop, and my uncle or the Icelander tried to help me. Fortunately our road was mostly downhill. It would have been impossible for me to climb.

At last, on Wednesday, the 8th of July, crawling along on our hands and knees, half dead with thirst, we got to the place where the two passages met. It was ten o'clock in the morning. I was no longer able to move at all. I lay there as if I were dead. I fell into a deep sleep.

After a little, my uncle came to me and, lifting me in his arms, said in a very gentle voice:

" My poor boy! "

I had never heard my uncle speak to me like that before. I took his shaking hand and held it in mine. He let me do it, and looked at me with tears in his eyes.

I saw him take the water-bottle and hold it towards me, while he said:

"Drink! "

How was this? What did he mean? Was my uncle mad? I could not understand him.

"Drink! " he said again.

I took the bottle and drank. Yes, it was water. It was only a mouthful but it was enough to bring back life to me.

I held my hands together as I thanked my uncle.

"Yes," he said, " a mouthful of water! The last, do you hear? The last. I kept it specially for you. Twenty times—no, a hundred times, I had to fight with myself to stop myself from drinking it; but no, Axel, I kept the last mouthful of water for you."

"Oh, uncle!" I said, and big tears came into my eyes.

"Yes, my poor boy, I knew that when you came to these cross roads you would drop down half dead, and I kept the last of the water for this moment."

"Thanks, thanks!" I cried.

"Well," I said, "there is now only one thing for us to do, and that is to go back."

My uncle kept his eyes away from me. He seemed ashamed to meet my eyes.

"We must go back," I cried, "and find our way to Sneffel. May we have enough strength to climb to the top of the mountain!"

"Go back?" said my uncle, speaking to himself, it seemed, more than to me.

"Yes, go back without wasting another moment."

For some time neither of us spoke.

Then, in a strange voice, the professor said:

"Well then, Axel, that little water has not made you any braver."

"Braver?"

"I see you are still without hope."

"What!" I cried. "Do you mean to say that you are not willing to try to get back?"

"Shall I give up the journey," answered my uncle, "at the very moment when everything promises success? Never!"

"Then we must be ready to die!"

"No, Axel, no! Start off back! Let Hans go with you. Leave me behind!"

"Leave you behind?"

"Yes, I tell you; leave me here. I have begun the journey, and I will finish it or never go back at all. Go, Axel, go!"

My uncle was very excited. His voice, which had become soft and gentle for a few moments, now sounded hard and angry. He was fighting with himself against impossibilities. I could not leave him here alone.

The guide looked at us all the time without showing any interest. He understood what was happening, all the same.

Our movements showed him that each of us was trying to make the other take a different road. It did not matter to Hans what we decided. He was ready to go on if my uncle made him the sign to go, and he was ready to stay if my uncle wished him to do so.

How I wanted to speak to him and make him understand me! I wanted him to join with me in forcing the professor to go back. I went up to him and laid my hand on his. He did not move. I pointed to the way back to the crater. He did not move. I tried to pull him. The Icelander gently shook his head and quietly pointing to my uncle, said:

" Master! "

" Master! " I cried. " He is not the master of your life. We must go back and we must make him come back with us. Do you understand? "

I had taken hold of his arm and was trying to pull him up. But my uncle said:

" Be calm, Axel! You will do nothing with that man. Listen, then, to what I have to say."

I looked at my uncle straight in the face.

" The want of water," he said, " is the only thing that is stopping us. In this passage to the east, made of lava, other rocks and coal, we have found no water at all. It is possible that we shall be more fortunate if we go along the one on the west."

I shook my head.

" Hear me to the end," said the professor. " While you were lying there without movement, I did what I ought to have done before. I went to examine the passage. It leads straight into the heart of the earth, and in a few hours we shall reach the rocks that have water running through them. It is the road taken by Arne Saknussemm. He needed water as much as we need it. He must have found water. Where he found it, we shall find it. Now this is what I am going to say. When Columbus was on his way to discover new countries, his men wanted to go back. He asked them to go on three days longer. They agreed, and he discovered the New World. I am the Columbus here, and I ask you to give me not three days more, but one day more. If we have not discovered water by that time, I promise you that we will go back to the place from where we started."

I could not help feeling that what my uncle said was reasonable.

"Very well," I said. "I agree, and may God reward you for your strength of mind and patience. You have a few hours to prove that you are right, so let us start at once."

9

LOWER STILL

W E made our way down the new passage, Hans walking on first, as usual. We had not gone a hundred steps when the professor, throwing the light of his lamp on the wall, cried:

"These are the right rocks. We have made no mistake this time. Forward! Forward! "

By eight o'clock in the evening we had found no sign of water. In spite of being so terribly tired, I walked on as well as I could. I did not want to make my uncle stop.

At last I had no strength left. I cried out: "I'm dying! Come to me," and then I fell flat on the ground. My uncle turned back and looked at me. Then I heard him say:

"This finishes it." I saw him make a movement of terrible anger, and then I shut my eyes.

When I opened my eyes again, I saw my two companions lying without movement. Were they asleep? As for myself, I could not get a moment's sleep. I was suffering too much. And I knew, too, that there was nothing to be done, that nothing could help us. And I thought, like my uncle:

"This finishes it."

For now there could be no question of going back. Six solid miles of rock lay between us and the world above us. I seemed to feel the weight of it.

Some hours passed. There was nothing to be heard.

No sound of any sort could reach us through these walls.

And yet, presently, I thought I heard a noise. It was dark in the passage, but looking closely I seemed to see the Icelander leaving us, with a lamp in his hand.

Why was he going? Was Hans really leaving us? My uncle was asleep. I tried to call out, but my voice could not make itself heard. It was now quite dark, and there was no more sound.

" Hans has left us! " I cried. " Hans, Hans! "

But these words were spoken inside me. They never came out of my mouth. The next moment I felt ashamed of myself for doubting him. If he had left us, it must be for some good reason. He was not going up the passage, but down it. That was a good sign and not a bad one. These thoughts made me feel more calm, and then other ideas came to me. What was the reason for his going off like that? Had he heard something that my uncle and I had not heard?

For a whole hour I was trying to imagine why Hans had gone, and what he was doing. The most foolish ideas came into my head. I thought I was going mad.

At last the noise of footsteps was heard in the depths of the passage. Hans was coming up again. The light began to shine on the walls again. Hans came in sight. He went up to my uncle, put his hand on his arm and gently woke him up. My uncle sat up and asked what was the matter.

" *Vatten,*" answered the guide.

Although I knew no Danish, I understood at once what he meant.

"Water! Water! " I cried.

"Water! " said my uncle. " *Hvar?* " he asked.

" *Nedat!* " answered Hans.

"Where? Down below! " I understood every word. I took hold of our guide's hands and pressed them, but he looked at me with perfect calmness.

We were soon ready, and walked down the passage.

In about an hour we had gone down 2,000 feet.

Then I heard an unusual sound of something inside the walls of rock. What was it?

I was beginning to give up hope again when we had walked for another half-hour and no water appeared. But my uncle told me that Hans was not mistaken, and that the noise we heard was that of running water.

" It is a river," he said.

" A river? "

" Yes, there is no doubt about it. An underground river is running close beside us."

We walked more quickly. The sound of the water made me feel better. It grew louder. At every moment I expected to see the water burst out.

Another half-hour passed, and three miles more.

It was clear that Hans could not have gone farther than this while he was away. It soon became clear, too, that if we went farther we should be going away from the water, for the noise was no longer so loud.

We turned back.

Hans stopped at the place where the water seemed nearest.

I sat down beside the wall, the water rushing along with great violence less than two feet from me, but with the wall of rock between. Instead of thinking of the best thing to do, I lost hope once again.

Hans looked at me, and I had the idea that he smiled.

He got up and took the lamp. I followed him. He went to the wall, laid his head against it and listened. Then he moved to a different place and listened again. He was clearly trying to find the exact part where the water made the most noise. At last he seemed to find it in the side wall to the left, about three feet from the ground.

I felt very excited. What was he going to do? I could not guess.

But I soon came to understand, when he lifted up his pick to strike the rock.

" Saved! " I cried.

" Yes! " cried my uncle with great joy, " Hans is right! Ah, the clever fellow! We should never have thought of that! "

I quite believe it. Such a plan, simple as it was, would

never have come into our heads. And yet it seemed a dangerous plan. Suppose the passage fell in and buried us? And what if this river should burst through and wash us away?

Never mind. We must have the water.

Hans did the work, for neither my uncle nor I could have done it. We should have been too impatient. The guide, however, was quite calm, and wore away the rock gradually until he had made an opening about six inches wide. I could hear the noise getting louder, and I seemed already to be drinking the water.

Soon the hole was two feet deep. Hans had already been at work for over an hour. I waited with impatience. My uncle was more impatient than I. Suddenly a stream of water burst out with great violence and struck against the opposite wall.

Hans, who was almost thrown over by the shock, gave a cry of pain, the reason for which I soon understood, and I, too, called out in pain when I found, by putting my hands into the water, that it was almost boiling.

" It's hot water! " I cried.

" Never mind," said my uncle. " It will get cold."

The passage was filled with steam, and a stream was formed that began to run down the tunnel. Soon we were able to take our first drink.

How can I describe that wonderful moment? Only those who have suffered severely from thirst for many days can understand how we felt. Oh, how good it was to drink! It did not matter what the water was nor where it had come from. It was water, and although still warm, it brought back life to us. I drank it without stopping, without even tasting.

But after a few moments I cried. " Why, it tastes of iron! "

" Splendid," said my uncle. " Very good for the health."

" Oh, it's good, isn't it? "

" Yes, it ought to be good, too. Water that comes from six miles under the ground! It tastes of iron, but it's a pleasant taste. Oh, it's really wonderful water that Hans has found for us, so we will give his name to this health-giving stream."

"Yes, certainly," I said. And this river was at once named *Hansbach*, meaning Hans Stream.

Hans was not in the least proud about it. He sat down in a corner with his usual calmness.

"Now," said I, "we must not let this water run away."

"Why not?" asked my uncle. "It will keep running all the time. It won't stop."

"All the same," I said, "let us fill up our bottles, and then try to stop up the hole."

My advice was followed. With some rope and stone we tried to stop up the hole. But it was not so easy to do it. The hot water was extremely painful to our hands, and in the end we did not succeed. The pressure was too great.

"It is clear," I said, "that the water must come from a long way up; if we are to judge by the force with which it comes out."

"There is no doubt of it," answered my uncle. "But I have an idea."

"What is it?"

"Why should we be so anxious to stop up this hole?"

"Because——"

Here I stopped, for it was not easy to find a reason.

"When our bottles are empty again," my uncle went on, "how do we know for certain that we shall be able to fill them?"

"That's true."

"Well, then, let the stream run down naturally. It will be our guide on the way, and will give us water as often as we want it."

"That's a splendid idea," I cried, "and with this stream for our companion, there is no reason why we should not succeed."

"Ah! you are coming to the right way of thinking, my boy," said the professor, laughing.

"I am doing better than coming; I *have* come. Let us start."

"Not yet," said my uncle. "We must have a few hours' rest."

I had forgotten that it was night.

After a good meal we lay down and were soon all three asleep.

The next day we had already forgotten our past sufferings. I was surprised at first, when I woke up, not to feel thirsty, and wondered what the reason could be. The stream running at my feet gave me a good answer.

We had breakfast and drank some of this good water. I felt very happy. Why should not a man like my uncle succeed, when he had a guide such as Hans, and a companion such as myself? If anyone had talked of going back to Sneffel, I should have refused angrily.

All we had to do was to keep going down.

"Come along! Let's start!" I cried out.

So we started again on Thursday, the 9th of July, at eight o'clock in the morning. The passage turned this way and that, bending to the right and to the left. My uncle looked at his compass almost all the time, to make certain in which direction we were going. This passage—or road—hardly went down at all. The stream ran at our feet. My uncle, of course, was impatient. He wanted the road to go down and down.

On the whole, that day and the next we went very far, but without going very far downwards.

On Friday, the 10th of July, we seemed to be eighty-five miles to the south-east of Reykjavik, and seven miles deep.

That evening we were about ninety miles to the south-east of Reykjavik, and about seven and a half miles deep. Here there appeared in front of us an immense hole that seemed to have no bottom to it. A terrible sight, indeed, but my uncle was extremely pleased to see it.

"Splendid," he cried. "This will take us a long way, and we shall have no trouble. The rocks standing out from the sides all the way are just like stairs."

We arranged the ropes as before, and began to go down. It was not difficult or dangerous, and I was getting used to that sort of work. The steps were regular, and looked almost as if they had been made by man.

Every quarter of an hour we stopped for a short rest. We sat down, eating and talking, and drinking the water of our stream, which was now a waterfall in most places. It came down so violently that it made me think of my uncle when he was angry, while before, when it was running calmly and slowly, it made me think of the Icelander.

On the 11th and 12th of July we were still going down these natural stairs, and by the evening of the 12th we had reached a farther depth of six miles. We were now nearly fifteen miles below the surface of the earth. But the next day the passage, although still going towards the south-east, no longer went down so steeply. The road now became easier, but it was not very interesting. Hour after hour we walked in the same way.

On Wednesday, the 15th, we were twenty-one miles under the earth and a hundred and fifty from Sneffel. Although rather tired we were in perfect health.

My uncle wrote down, every hour, particulars of our journey; the exact time, the temperature, the depth and the direction. In this way we always knew where we were. When he told me that we had gone a hundred and fifty miles to the south-east, I felt some surprise.

" Uncle."

" What is it, my boy? "

" I was just thinking. If you are right, we are no longer below Iceland."

" Do you think so? "

" We can find out at once."

I took the map and made some measurements, and found that I was quite right.

" We have passed Cape Portland," I said, " and 120 miles south-east brings us to the open sea."

" Splendid," said my uncle.

" Then the sea is really above our heads? "

The professor saw nothing wonderful in the fact, but my mind was quite excited with the idea of walking below the sea. And yet what difference did it make whether the mountains of Iceland were over our heads, or the waves of the Atlantic? It was all the same to us, for all we could see was the solid rock through which we were passing. I soon got used to the thought, for the passage, whether running straight or turning to the left or right, was leading us towards the centre of the earth.

Four days later, on Saturday, the 18th of July, in the evening, we reached a rather large cave. Here we stopped, and my uncle paid Hans for the week. It was agreed that the next day should be a day of rest.

I woke up the next morning, then, without the usual feeling of having to start off again at once. Although we were in the deepest depths, it was not unpleasant. We were quite ready for this life underground. I hardly thought of the sun, or stars, or the moon, or trees, or houses, or towns.

The stream ran over the rocky bed of the cave. At this distance from the place that it burst out of the rock, it was not even warm.

After breakfast, the professor decided to spend a few hours in examining and arranging his papers.

" First," he said, " I am going to find out exactly where we are. I wish to be able, when we get back, to make a map of our journey."

" That would be a valuable thing, uncle; but could you make it with enough exactness? "

" Yes, I have carefully noticed everything; the degree of steepness of our road, and its direction. We have now gone 255 miles from our starting-point, and 48 miles down."

" Forty-eight miles down? "

" Yes, there's no doubt about that."

" But, according to science, the solid part of the earth is only 48 miles deep."

" Yes. Well? "

" And if the heat increases one degree in 70 feet, the heat here ought to be 1,500 degrees."

" Ought to be, my boy."

" But at that heat, the rock ought to be melting and running like water. It could not possibly be solid."

" But it is solid, as you see, and there is no truth in the belief in the heat in the centre of the earth."

" I have to admit it, but I am very much surprised at it."

" What does the thermometer say? "

" Twenty-seven and six-tenths."

" So you see Humphry Davy was right, and I was right to listen to him."

" Uncle," I said, " what you have said seems to be right. But all the same there is one fact of very great importance that we must not forget."

" And what is it, my boy? Speak freely."

" It is 4,750 miles from the surface of Iceland to the centre of the earth."

" Quite so."

" Let us call it 4,800 miles. Out of a journey of 4,800 miles we have gone 48."

" Yes."

" And we have had to walk 255 miles to get to this depth."

" Quite right."

" In about twenty days."

" In twenty days."

" Now 48 miles is the hundredth part of 4,800 miles. If we go on at this rate, the journey will take us 2,000 days, or nearly five and a half years."

My uncle did not answer.

" Again," I went on. " We have had to walk 255 miles sideways in order to get 48 miles down, and so, at this rate, we shall have to walk 24,000 miles south-east. It's a long way to the centre of the earth."

" How do you know that your figures are right? " cried my uncle, angrily. " What makes you think that the rest of our journey is going to be like the first twenty days of it? How do you know that this passage does not lead straight to the centre of the earth? Besides, what we are doing some-one has already done; and where he has succeeded, we shall succeed too."

D

"I hope so; but at least I may be allowed to——"

"To say nothing more, Axel, if you wish to talk in this foolish way."

I saw that my gentle uncle was changing into the terrible professor, and I thought it better to say no more.

"Now," he said, "look at the barometer. What does it show?"

"A heavy pressure."

"Well, then, you see that by going down little by little we are getting used to the weight of the air. You don't suffer by it?"

"No, except for a little pain in the ears."

"That's nothing, and it will go away at once if you breathe quickly for a minute."

"Quite so," I said. "It is quite pleasant breathing this heavy air. Have you noticed how wonderfully clear the sound is?"

"Yes, I have."

"The air will keep getting heavier as we go on, won't it?"

"Yes, it will make a difference to the weight of things. It is on the surface of the earth that things are heaviest, at the centre of the earth they will have no weight at all."

"Then, uncle, at a certain depth the air will be as heavy as water."

"Yes, of course it will."

"And lower still?"

"Lower still it will get heavier."

"Then how shall we be able to go down through it?"

"Well, we must put stones into our pockets!"

My uncle always had an answer for everything.

But it was quite clear that at a certain depth the air would become solid, and I could not imagine myself walking through solid air. It was no good saying this to my uncle; it would only make him angry again, and he would have talked of Saknussemm. Saknussemm! In the sixteenth century the barometer had not been invented, so how could he have known that he had reached the centre of the earth?

10

LOST

O N the Monday morning we started off again.

For some days the road went downwards very steeply, so steeply, indeed, that we walked with some difficulty. On some days we went from four to six miles. Hans was of great help to us. In fact without him I do not know how we should have got on.

During the two weeks that followed our last talk nothing particular happened.

On the 7th of August we were ninety miles below the surface of the earth, and we must have been six hundred miles away from Iceland.

That day the passage was not at all steep. I was in front of the others with one of the lamps. Suddenly, on turning round, I found myself alone.

"All right," I thought. "I have been going too fast, or Hans and uncle may have stopped for a minute on the road. I must get back to them. Fortunately the road is not steep."

I walked back along the way I had come, and, a quarter of an hour later, I looked round me. Nobody was in sight. I called out. No answer.

I began to feel frightened.

"Be calm," I said to myself aloud. "I am sure of finding them again. There are not two roads. I was walking in front, so I must just keep going back."

I went back for half an hour longer, and then I listened to hear if anyone called me. There was not a sound.

I stopped. I could not believe that I was really alone. I had lost my way; I should find my way again after a time.

"There is only the one passage," I kept saying to myself, "and as they are in it, I must come to them soon. I have only to keep walking up. Unless, not seeing me, and forgetting I was in front, they have gone back to look for me. But even then, by hurrying, I shall catch them up, that's clear."

I said these last words like a man who is not very certain, and it took me a long time to put my ideas together at all in the form of clear reasoning, simple as they were.

Then a doubt came over me. Was I really in front of my companions when I saw them last? Certainly I was. Hans was following me, and my uncle came after him. He had even stopped a moment to fasten his bundle on his shoulder. I remembered this clearly. It was at this very moment that I must have gone on too far.

" Besides," thought I, " it is impossible I could have gone far wrong, for I have a guide to lead me; one that will never leave me—the stream. I have only to follow it back and I cannot help finding my companions."

This thought made me feel brave again, and I decided to start off at once, without wasting a moment.

How thankful I was at the wisdom of my uncle now, in not allowing Hans to stop up the hole from which the water had first burst out! This stream was now to be my guide through the passages under the earth.

Before starting I thought I should feel better if I had a wash. I bent down to put my hands in the stream, but imagine how much I was surprised and frightened! I touched dry rock. The stream no longer ran at my feet!

I cannot describe my terrible state of mind. I was buried alive, and must at last die of cold and hunger and thirst.

I passed my hands over the ground. How dry the rock seemed!

But could I have left the bed of the stream? For it was certainly not here. Now I understood the cause of this strange quietness, when I listened the last time for a call from my companions. I had not, till this moment, noticed that the stream was not there. It was clear that just as I took the first step in the wrong direction, the tunnel must have divided into two, and I had followed the new opening, while the Hansbach had followed the other and had gone away with my companions towards unknown depths. How could I get back? There was nothing to guide me, not even my

own footsteps. I thought and thought so that I might find some way to save myself. But no! I was lost!

Yes, lost at what seemed to me to be a depth too great to measure or even to think of.

I tried to bring my thoughts back to the upper world. But I hardly succeeded. Hamburg, the house in which I lived—all the world beneath which I was lost passed quickly before my memory. I seemed to see all the happenings of our journey—the voyage, Iceland, Mr Fridriksson, Sneffel! I said to myself that to have any hope would be foolish, and that I had far better give up all hope.

What could bring me back again to the surface of the earth? Who could put me in the right path once more, and take me to join my companions again?

"Oh, uncle!" I cried in my unhappiness, and I knew how much the poor man would suffer while he was looking for me without success.

When I saw myself in this way quite cut off from help, from my companions, and unable to do anything for myself, I thought of help from God. Memories of my mother, whom I had known only in the sweet days when I was very young, came back to me. I began to pray.

This cry for help made me calm, and I was able to bring all my mind to think over my true position.

I had food and water enough for three days. It would be foolish of me to stay any longer where I was, but which way should I go? Should I go up or down?

Go up, of course—always keep going up. I must then surely come to the point where the passage had divided, and if I could only find the stream again I could get back to the surface of the earth.

How was it that I had not thought of this before? There was clearly some possibility of escape here. My first business was to find the Hansbach again.

I stood up, and began again to climb. The road was rather steep, but I walked on hopefully like a man who has not the choice of roads before him.

For half an hour I found no difficulty. I tried to find the way by the shape of the tunnel and certain rocks, and the arrangement of the cracks. But I remembered nothing, and I soon saw that this road would not bring me to the place where I had taken the wrong turning. My tunnel came to an end; there was no further road. I struck against a wall of rock and fell to the ground.

What terrible fear took hold of me then, I cannot describe. My last hope was broken against this wall of rock.

Lost among passages and rocks, it was useless to try to save myself. The most terrible of deaths was before me.

I tried to speak aloud but could form no words. I could hardly breathe.

Then a new fear took hold of me. My lamp had gone wrong when I fell. I could not put it right, and its light was getting weaker and would soon go out. I saw the light getting weaker and weaker. I did not dare shut my eyes, for fear that I might lose the last of the little light that was left. Every moment it looked as if it would go out and leave me in the blackness of night.

At last there was only the weakest light. I looked at it with anxiety, until nothing more was to be seen.

What a terrible cry burst from me! On the earth, even in the darkess night, there is always some light, weak as it may be. Here there was nothing.

Then I lost my senses. I got up with my arms stretched out, trying to feel my way, but it was most painful to do so. I ran along madly through the passages, always going down deeper into the heart of the earth, calling, crying, striking myself against rocks, falling down and getting up again, feeling the blood running, and trying to drink it as it dropped from my face, and always expecting to come to some wall to knock my head against.

In what direction did I go? That I do not know, and shall never know.

After several hours, no doubt, when all my strength was at an end, I fell against the wall like a lifeless mass, and lost all knowledge of anything.

When I became conscious again, my face was wet—wet with tears. How long I had been in that state I cannot say, I had no longer any way of counting the hours. Never had loneliness been like mine or so complete.

After my fall I lost a quantity of blood—I felt it all over me.

Oh, how sorry I was that death was still to come! I would not let myself think, and in my hopeless state I rolled myself towards the opposite wall.

I could feel myself ready to become unconscious again, and I thought with satisfaction that when I did so it would be for ever, and I should never wake again. A loud noise struck my ear. It was like a burst of rolling thunder; it grew less and died away in the distance.

Where did the noise come from? No doubt from some place deep down in the earth. The explosion of some gas, or the fall of some of the earth's rocks.

I listened again. I wanted to know whether that noise

would be heard again. A quarter of an hour passed. Nothing was to be heard but the beating of my heart.

Suddenly my ear, which happened to touch the wall, was surprised by a sound like distant words—words without meaning to me, but, all the same words. I shook with excitement.

" Is it my imagination? " thought I.

But no! I listened more carefully, and then I could clearly hear the low sound of voices, but I was too weak to understand what was said; but I was certain that someone was speaking. I again put my ear near the wall.

Yes! Yes! Voices without any doubt!

I crept to some distance along the wall, and then heard the sounds more clearly. I seemed to be hearing meaningless words. They sounded as if someone were singing them in a low voice. Once or twice I caught the word *" forlorad "*.[1]

What did it mean? Who was speaking? Either my uncle or Hans. But, if I could hear *them*, surely they might hear *me*!

" Here," I called with all my strength. " Here! "

I listened. I listened in the darkness for an answer. Not a sound. I had the idea that my voice could not reach my companions.

" For it is certainly they," said I. " What other men would there be here, ninety miles underground? "

I listened again. In trying backwards and forwards along the wall I found a place where the voices seemed to be clearest and loudest. The word *" forlorad "* again reached my ear, and the loud noise that I had first heard.

" No! " I cried; " it is not through this rock that I hear the voices. The wall is of solid rock, and the loudest sound could not come through it. The sound comes by way of the passage itself."

I listened once more. Yes! this time I heard my own name through the darkness!

It was my uncle who had said the word! He was, of course,

---

[1] A Danish word meaning " lost ".

talking to Hans, and the word *"forlorad"* was a Danish word.

Then I understood it all. To make them hear me, all I had to do was to speak with my mouth close to the wall, which would carry my voice to them.

But I had no time to waste. If my companions happened to change their position, even by a few steps, they would not be able to hear me. I went close to the wall, and I said, slowly and loudly:

"Uncle Lidenbrock!"

And I waited anxiously. Sound does not travel quickly here. The air is heavy, much heavier than on the surface of the earth, and heaviness makes sound louder but does not make it go fast. A few moments passed, and at last I heard these words:

"Axel! Axel! Is that you?"

"Yes! yes!" I answered.

"My boy, where are you?"

"Lost in the blackest darkness."

"Where is your lamp?"

"Out!"

"And the stream?"

"Gone!"

"Axel, my poor boy: be brave!"

"Just wait a little. I'm too tired to speak. I haven't got strength to answer. But talk to me!"

"Very well," said my uncle. "Don't speak: listen to me. We went up and down the passage, looking for you. We couldn't find you. Tears came from my eyes, my boy! Then we came down again, firing our guns as we came, always supposing you still in the passage where the stream runs. We thought you must hear the sound of our guns. Now that our voices meet it is by accident, and we cannot touch hands. But do not lose hope, Axel. It is good that we can even hear each other."

 .   .   .   .

During this time I had been thinking. A little hope, a very little hope, indeed, made me feel braver. First of all, it was necessary for me to know one thing. I put my mouth to the wall and said:
"Uncle?"

 .   .   .   .

"My boy!" he replied after several seconds had passed.

 .   .   .   .

"We must first find out what distance there is between us."

 .   .   .   .

"That is easy."

 .   .   .   .

"You have your watch?"

 .   .   .   .

"Yes."

 .   .   .   .

"Well, take it! Call my name, and note the exact moment. I will call it the moment I hear it, and you will again note the exact moment."

 .   .   .   .

"Yes! and half the time between the question and the answer will be the time needed for my voice to reach you."

 .   .   .   .

"Just so, uncle!"

 .   .   .   .

"Are you ready?"

 .   .   .   .

"Yes."

 .   .   .   .

" Well, listen now; I am going to call out your name! "

I put my ear to the wall, and as soon as the word " Axel " reached me, I at once answered " Axel ", and then waited.

" Forty seconds! " said my uncle. " Therefore the sound took twenty seconds to come to you. Now, at the rate of 1,020 feet a second, that makes 20,400 feet, or nearly four miles."

" Nearly four miles," I cried, with an unhappy voice

" Well, that's not an impossible distance, Axel! "

" But must I go up or down? "

" Down and for this reason—we have come to an immense open place into which several passages run. The one you have got into must lead here, for I feel certain that all these passages, or cracks in the earth, run out of the great cave in which Hans and I are standing. Be brave and come on. Walk, creep, slip down the steep passage, if necessary, and you will find our strong arms waiting to support you at the end. Forward, my boy, forward! "

These words filled me with new life.

" Good-bye, uncle," I cried; " I'm coming. When I leave this spot, we can no longer speak to each other."

" Till we meet again, Axel! "

I heard nothing more.

This strange talk, carried on in the great depths of the earth at a distance of nearly four miles, ended with words of hope. I thanked God for having led me through the darkness to the only point at which the voices of my companions could reach me.

What had happened was easily explained; the shape and arrangement of the passage had carried our voices to each other. There are many examples of very low sounds being sent to great distances. I have known such cases, once inside St. Paul's Cathedral in London, and in those strange caves in Sicily, and in the underground passages near Syracuse in Sicily.

These memories came to my mind, and it seemed clear that, as my uncle's voice reached me, there could be nothing to prevent us from meeting again. If I went along the road by which the sound came, it would be impossible for me not to reach him if I were not stopped by weakness.

I got up—I crept more than walked. The road was very steep, and I let myself slip down. After a little, the road got steeper and steeper, and my downward movement seemed likely to become a falling movement. I had no strength to stop myself.

Suddenly my feet slipped and I fell. I felt myself rolling, and now and then striking against the rocks sticking out from the walls. My head struck against a sharp point of rock, and I lost consciousness.

When I became conscious again I found myself in a place that was nearly dark. My uncle was looking at me, hoping for a sign of life in my face. When I first moved he took my hand; when I opened my eyes he cried out in a happy voice:

" He's alive! he's alive! "

" Yes," I answered, weakly.

" My boy! " said my uncle, pressing me to his heart. " Thank God you are saved! "

My feelings were deeply touched by the way in which my uncle said these words.

Then Hans came up to us. He saw my hand in that of my uncle. I may say at least that his eyes showed great satisfaction.

" *God dag*," said he.

" Good day, Hans," I said, in a low voice. " And now, uncle, tell me where we are."

"Tomorrow, Axel, tomorrow; today you are too weak. You have hurt your head, but I have seen to it, and done all that is necessary. You must try to sleep now, and tomorrow you shall hear all that I have to tell you."

"Well," said I, "at least tell me what time it is—or what day it is."

"Eleven o'clock in the evening, and today is Sunday, the 9th of August, and I will answer no more questions until the 10th of this month."

I was really weak, and went to sleep at once.

I I

A HUNDRED MILES DOWN

THE next day, when I woke up, I looked round.

My bed, made of all the travelling rugs, was in the middle of a beautiful cave. The ground was covered with clean, white sand. The lamps were not burning, but there was a sort of light that came in by a narrow opening. I could hear, too, a sound as if I were listening to the waves of the sea breaking on the sands, and at times I heard the sound of a gentle wind.

I wondered whether I was really awake or still dreaming. Or was it that the knock that I had received on my head made me imagine such things? Still, neither my eyes nor my ears could be so mistaken.

"It is really daylight," I thought, "that is coming in through that crack. And I am sure that the sounds that I hear are the sounds of waves and wind. What does it mean? Are we once more on the surface of the earth? Has my uncle given up the idea of going to the centre of the earth, or what?"

I was asking myself these questions, to which I could find no answer, when my uncle came in.

" Good morning, Axel," he said, in a happy voice. " I am certain that you are much better."

"Yes, I am," I said, sitting up.

"That's right. That's splendid. You have been sleeping quietly. Sometimes I sat by your side, and sometimes Hans, and we have been seeing you get better little by little."

"In fact, uncle, I feel quite a man again; and you will agree with me when you see how much breakfast I shall eat —at least, if you give me any breakfast."

"Certainly, my boy; you shall eat. Your head is much better."

As I ate my breakfast I asked my uncle many questions, which he did his best to answer.

He told me that my fall had brought me to the end of a very steep passage. I had come down together with a great number of stones, the smallest of which would have been enough to crush me.

"I am really surprised," he said, "that you were not killed a thousand times. But we must never separate again."

"Never separate again?" Then the journey was not over.

"What's the matter, Axel?"

"I want to ask you a question. You say that I am all right?"

"Certainly. There's nothing the matter with you."

"There's nothing wrong with my head?"

"Nothing at all."

"And yet I think that my head is not right. Are we not on the surface of the earth?"

"No, we are not."

"Well, then, I am certainly mad. I see the light of day, I hear the wind blowing, and the waves of the sea breaking."

"Oh, is that all?"

"Well, but explain to me——"

"I will explain nothing, for I cannot explain anything. You must come and see for yourself, and then you will admit that geologists do not know much about what there is deep down in the earth."

"Let us go out, then," I said, getting up suddenly.

"No, Axel, no; the open air might be bad for you."

"The open air?"

"Yes; the wind is rather strong."

"But I tell you I am absolutely well."

"A little patience, my boy! It won't do for you to lose your strength again. We have no time to lose, because it may take a long time to go across."

"Across? Across what? What do you mean?"

"Yes, have another day's rest, and then we shall be ready for our journey by water."

"By water?"

The word made me jump.

What did he mean? Had we a river, a lake, a sea in front of us? Was there a ship somewhere?

I was strongly excited. My uncle tried to make me calm, but could not do so. When he saw that my excitement was making me worse instead of better, he agreed to let me go out.

I dressed quickly.

At first I could see nothing. There was too much light for my eyes. When I was able to open them, it was not that I was surprised; I could understand nothing at all.

"The sea!" I cried.

"Yes," said my uncle. "The sea. The Sea of Lidenbrock; that is its name. I think I may be allowed to call it by my own name."

A great stretch of water, the beginning of a lake or sea, went out farther than the eye could reach. The shore, of clean, white sand, went gently down into the water. A light wind was blowing. About 300 feet away from the edge of the water was the steep line of rocky coast. It was exactly as if we were on the surface of the earth. It was a real sea, a real shore, and there were real hills. The light was just like the light of day, but it was certainly not sunlight, nor moonlight. It was a white light, a white cold light. From where did it come? What made it?

There was a sky, too. It seemed to be covered with clouds, which at any time might fall as rain. But it could not be a real sky. I felt that above the clouds there must be an immense roof of volcanic rock, and it seemed to crush me with its weight. Yet it must have been at least nine miles above us. You can imagine from this the size of the cave.

What could have made this cave? Who knows? I have no words to describe all that I felt.

My uncle was already used to this sight, and showed no surprise.

"Are you ready for a little walk?" he asked.

"Yes, certainly," I answered, "I should like nothing better."

"Well, take my arm, Axel, and let us go along the shore."

I agreed, with pleasure. On the left were the mountains that formed the coast. Down their sides came waterfalls, and here and there ran streams of clear water. Among these I noticed our travelling companion, the Hansbach, which ran quietly into the sea, as if it had been doing nothing else since the world began.

"We shall be sorry to leave it now," said I.

"What does it matter," said the professor, "whether we have that or another? One stream is very much like another."

I thought his answer was rather ungrateful.

At this moment I saw something that I did not at all expect. Five hundred steps away was a forest, a forest of high trees. But what strange trees! They seemed to have no leaves, and they made no movement in spite of the wind. I went towards them. I could find no name for them. Were they trees of a different sort from any on the earth? No. When we reached them, my surprise was equal to my admiration. My uncle told me what they were.

"It is a forest of mushrooms,"[1] he said.

He was right. Imagine how high these may grow in such a place as this!

We walked among them for half an hour. They made the air cold.

[1] *Mushroom:* small, quick-growing, plant-like thing which does not, like plants, make its own food.

But these were not the only trees. Farther on we saw others: not trees that grow on the surface of the earth today, but those which used to grow there many millions of years ago.

It was a treasure-house of the past, this great cave. Not only a treasure-house of plants, but of the bones of animals. We saw them in thousands lying about. We saw the bones of those terrible animals that lived on the earth twenty or fifty million years ago.

But if such animals had lived down here, why should we not find one alive and walking among these dark forests or behind these steep rocks? As this idea came into my head, I looked round me with some fright, but no living animal was to be seen.

My walk made me a little tired. I went and sat down on a rock beside the sea. From here I could see the whole of the bay that stretched out in front of us. I almost expected to see ships and boats. But we were certainly the only living things in this lower world. All sorts of questions came to my mind. What was this sea? How far did it go? Should we ever see the other side of it?

The next day I woke up feeling absolutely well. I thought it would be a good thing for me to go for a swim in this *Mediterranean Sea*. For if *mediterranean* means " the middle of the earth ", this was certainly the best name for this sea.

I came back ready for a good breakfast.

" Now," said my uncle, " it is high tide."

" What, a tide? "

" Of course. Why should there not be high and low tides here, as on the surface of the earth? Here, as anywhere else, the water feels the pull of the sun and moon, and must obey it."

We went down to the shore. There was no doubt about it; the water was getting higher and higher.

" It is wonderful," I said.

" No," said my uncle, " not wonderful, but quite natural."

" In spite of that," I answered, " I think it is wonderful. In fact I can hardly believe my eyes. Who could have imagined that so far under the surface of the earth there should be a real sea with tides? "

" Why not? Is there any reason against it? "

" I know of none," I answered, " if you give up the idea of central heat."

" I have given it up," said my uncle. " I agree with Humphry Davy, as you know, that there is no central heat."

" Then if that is so, uncle, there may be seas and countries in the middle of the earth. But you have not yet told me exactly where we are."

" We are now," answered my uncle, " 1,050 miles from Iceland."

" So far? "

" Yes, I am certain."

" And how far are we down? "

" About a hundred miles."

" Well then," I said, after having looked at the map, " the mountains of Scotland are above us."

" Yes," said the professor, smiling. " There is a great weight to carry, but the roof is strong enough to carry it."

" Oh, I'm not afraid of the roof falling down. But now, uncle, what are your plans? Do you mean to go back now to the surface of the earth? "

" Go back? What an idea! Of course not, We will go on, more particularly as we have had such good fortune so far! "

" Still, I don't see how we are going to get below this water."

" As this sea is, after all, nothing but a lake, it must have land all round it."

" That is most probable," I answered.

" Well then, on the opposite shore I am certain to find a new passage."

" And how far across is it, do you think? "

" From 100 to 120 miles. So you see, we have no time to waste; we sail tomorrow."

I looked round, half expecting to find a ship waiting for us.

" Ah," I said, " so we sail tomorrow. On what ship? "
"Not on a ship at all, my boy, but on a strong safe raft."[1]

" A raft," I said in surprise, " but we can no more build a raft than a ship, and I don't see——"

" You don't see, Axel, but if you listened, you could hear Hans at work making it."

" Do you mean to tell me that Hans is making a raft? "

" I do."

" What? Has he cut down trees with his axe? "

" Oh, they did not need to be cut down. Come and look at him at work."

After a quarter of an hour's walking, and on the other side of some rocks that ran out into the sea, I could see Hans working at the raft. A few more steps, and I was at his side.

---

[1] *Raft:* lengths of wood fastened together to float on water.

To my great surprise a raft already half finished lay on the sand. It was made of a strange-looking wood.

"Uncle," I asked, "what kind of wood is that?"

"It is wood changed into stone by the sea water; it is fossil wood."

"Then it must be as hard as stone, and cannot float."

"Fossil wood is sometimes like that, but not always. But look for yourself," said my uncle, throwing into the water one of these pieces of wood.

It first sank, and then came up to the surface of the waves.

"Are you satisfied?" asked my uncle.

"It is not to be believed, but I am satisfied," was my answer.

The next evening at seven o'clock, through the cleverness of our guide, the raft was ready. It was ten feet long and five feet wide. Half an hour later it was floating quietly on the waters of the "Sea of Lidenbrock".

On the morning of August 13th we got up early. We were to start our new way of travelling—a quick and easy one. We had made a mast,[1] and by fastening a thinner piece of wood across it, we were able to put up a sail—which was one of our rugs. Hans had made an oar by which the raft could be guided. We had plenty of ropes, and the whole thing was very solid and well put together. We had put on it all our luggage, food and instruments, together with plenty of water.

At six o'clock the professor gave the order to start. Hans was at the guiding oar. I unfastened the rope that tied us to the shore. The wind blew from the north-west; and we moved quickly away from the land. The weight of the air gave unusual strength to the wind. After an hour's sailing we were able to form some idea of the rate at which we were travelling.

"If we go on like this," said my uncle, "we shall do about ninety miles in twenty-four hours, and shall soon get to the shore on the other side."

[1] *Mast:* thick piece of wood standing upright to carry sails.

Already the northern shore was beginning to sink out of sight, and a few hours later was no longer to be seen. We were in the open sea. Great clouds were moving above us.

Evening came, and, as I had noticed the day before, evening brought no darkness with it; day and night were the same.

Professor Lidenbrock had asked me to write down each day everything that happened, the direction of the wind, the rate at which we travelled, the distance travelled; in short, everything that could be of interest.

12

TERRIBLE DANGER

THE following is what I wrote in my note-book during the days we passed at sea.

"*Friday, August 14th*. Wind from the north-west. The raft is going fast, and in a straight line. We have left the coast ninety miles behind. Nothing is to be seen. No difference in the strength of the light. Weather fine—that is, the clouds are high and look the colour of silver. Thermometer 32 degrees."

At twelve o'clock Hans fastened a fish-hook to the end of a piece of rope, put a piece of meat on it and threw it into the sea. After two hours he had caught nothing. Then there were no fish in these waters. No! Something is pulling at the rope. Hans drew in the rope and found a fish at the end.

It had a flat, rounded head; the back part of its body was covered with bony plates; it had no eyes, no teeth and no tail.

" What a strange fish! " I cried.

The professor looked at it.

"Yes," said he: " it is a fish that stopped living in the seas on the surface of the earth long ago, one of the fish that you see among the fossils. It belongs to the *Devonian* age."

" What! " I cried, " we have caught a living fish that stopped living over a hundred million years ago? "

" Yes, that is what we have done," answered the professor with joy in his voice. " These fossil fish, as you know, are quite different from the fish that live now. To have caught a living one is a wonderful thing."

Hans tried again, and at the end of two hours we had caught a large number of fish of the same sort, and others of different sorts, but all of families which are no longer living. This unexpected catch was a welcome addition to our food.

It seemed certain, then, that the only fish living in this sea were those that are found on the surface of the earth above only in a fossil state. Was it not possible that we might meet with some of those terrible lizards[1] that used to live fifty million years ago?

Then my mind went into a sort of day-dream. I seemed to be back to the early stages of the earth. First the world without any life at all on it, no animals, no plants; an empty world, except for rocks and water. Then the beginnings of life (perhaps two hundred million years ago). Then the age of fishes, followed by the age of plants—the plants that gave us our coal. Then I thought of the age when immense land-lizards walked about the earth, and water-lizards swam in the seas and flying-lizards made their way through the air. And then, much later (perhaps only twenty million years ago), the age when the early forms appeared of animals that we know today—the first horses no larger than dogs, the first elephants. Then the first men, covered with hair and living in a wild state—like the animals themselves. And then, in the end, the great ice age, when most

[1] *Lizard:* animal with four short legs and a long tail. (Small lizards eat flies in houses in some countries.)

of Europe was covered by thick and deep mountains of ice.

But is there not the possibility, here in this underground world, of seeing with my own eyes, alive and real, the wonders of past ages?

I woke up from my day-dream, hearing my uncle say:

" Yes, a good wind and a calm sea, and, if I am right, it will not be long before we touch land."

I stood up. I looked round me, but saw nothing except the line of sea lost in the clouds.

Saturday, August 15th. Everything is just the same. No land in sight. Water all round us. We might be in the middle of the Atlantic or the Pacific Ocean.

I am feeling strangely excited. My uncle seems only angry. Why should he be angry?

I have already said that my uncle is an impatient man. But there seems nothing to make him impatient. Everything is going on well. Our journey is going on well, and the raft is sailing fast.

" What's the matter, uncle? "

" There is nothing the matter."

" Are you impatient? "

" Why should I be impatient? "

" We are travelling fast."

" Yes, we are travelling fast, but the sea is too wide."

I remembered that the professor had thought that the sea would be only a hundred miles from end to end. We had gone three times that distance, and the southern shore was not yet in sight.

" We are not going down," said the professor. " All this is wasted time."

" But if we have followed the road of Saknussemm——"

" That is the question that is troubling me. Have we followed his road? Did he find this sea? Did he cross it? Did the stream that we followed lead us in the right direction? "

" Well," I answered, " we have no reason for being sorry to have come as far as this. Everything is going on well."

" Yes, but we are not going any deeper."

At six o'clock Hans said that it was time for him to have his money for the week's work, and my uncle gave it to him.

Sunday, August 16th. Nothing new. Weather keeps just the same. Wind a little stronger. When I wake up, my first thought is about the light. I am always afraid that it will get less and less. But it is as bright as ever.

The sea seems to have no end to it. It must be as large as the Mediterranean, or even the Atlantic. Why not?

Several times my uncle has tried to find the depth. He fastened one of our heaviest picks to a rope 1,200 feet long and let it down into the water. He found no bottom! We had great difficulty in pulling up the rope. When the pick came up, Hans pointed to some strange marks on its surface.

"*Tander!*" he said.

I did not understand.

"Teeth," said my uncle.

Yes, it was certainly teeth that had made those marks. But with what a strength! Are some of those terrible animals living at the bottom of the sea? Was there truth in my dream? The thought frightened me.

Monday, August 17th. I cannot help thinking all the time about the tooth-marks on the pick. I looked at the sea and was afraid that at any time one of these terrible animals might come in sight.

I suppose Professor Lidenbrock had the same idea, for when he had examined the pick he looked carefully at the sea.

I examined our guns to make certain that they were in good order. My uncle noticed me doing so, and smiled to show that we were both thinking the same thing.

Sometimes we saw a strange movement on the surface of the water. That looked like danger. We must be careful.

Tuesday, August 18th. Evening came, or rather there came the moment when we felt sleepy. Hans was at the oar and keeping watch, and I went to sleep.

Two hours later a terrible shock woke me up. The raft was lifted off the water and thrown on the waves again a hundred feet away.

" What's the matter? " cried my uncle. " Have we struck against a rock? "

Hans pointed to a dark body about twelve hundred feet away, which moved upwards and downwards. I looked, and then called out, " It is an immense fish! "

" Yes," said my uncle, " and there is a sea-lizard of uncommon size."

" And beyond that a great crocodile! Look at its teeth! Ah! it has gone! "

" A whale![1] a whale! " cried the professor. " See the air and water shooting up into the air! "

We stood surprised and helpless, in great fear of these animals. They were of an immense size, and the smallest of them could have bitten our raft in two with its teeth. Hans wanted to turn to one side to escape; but on that side new animals came in sight; a turtle[2] forty feet long, a snake thirty feet long, which moved its great head this way and that way high above the waves.

It was impossible to escape. The animals were coming nearer; they moved round and round us. I took one of the guns. But after all, what would be the use of it? for the bodies of these animals had a skin as hard as iron.

We were so frightened that we could not say a word. They came nearer; the crocodile on one side, the snake on the other. The rest of the animals were no longer to be seen. I was just going to shoot, but Hans stopped me. The animals were only about three hundred feet away from the raft. They jumped at each other, and the fight started. In their anger, fortunately, they did not notice us. But as I looked at them, it seemed as if the other animals came and joined in the fight—the great fish, the whale, the lizard, the turtle. I saw them all. I pointed them out to Hans. He shook his head.

" *Tva!* " said he.

" What? Two? He says there are only two! "

---

[1] *Whale:* the largest sea-animal.
[2] *Turtle:* sea-animal with four legs and a shell.

"He is right," said my uncle.

"You can't mean it, uncle!"

"Yes, I mean it. One of them has the mouth of a great fish, the head of a lizard, the teeth of a crocodile. It is the most terrible of all the sea-lizards—the *ichthyosaurus*!"

"And the other?"

"The other, with a body like a turtle and a neck like a snake, is the *plesiosaurus*!"

Hans was right. Only two animals were there, and they were both out of the middle of the ages of the earth.

These animals fought with unbelievable violence; they sent up waves like mountains. An hour passed; two hours passed: the battle still went on. Sometimes the fighters came in our direction, and sometimes they moved away. All that we could do was to look on.

Suddenly the two animals went out of sight down into the depths of the sea. Some minutes passed. Was the fight still going on down below?

All at once a head shot up out of the water—the head of the *plesiosaurus*. The great creature is badly wounded; it is throwing its long neck up and down, round and round. But before long the movements are not so violent, and a little after that the long neck lies on the surface of the water and the animal is lifeless.

As for the *ichthyosaurus*, we wondered whether it had gone back to its home under the sea or whether we should see it again on the surface.

Wednesday, August 19th. Fortunately the wind, which is blowing pretty strongly, made it possible to get away with good speed from this dangerous place. Hans is still at the oar. My uncle has become impatient again, and looks out all the time, wondering when we shall see land again. Our journey is uninteresting—except at the time of danger, and then it is too interesting.

Thursday, August 20th. Wind from the north-north-east. Temperature hot. We are going about nine and a half miles an hour.

Towards the middle of the day we heard a very distant

sound. I note the fact here without being able to explain what it is. It is a roar that goes on all the time.

"There must be in the distance," said the professor, "some rocks or island on which the sea breaks."

Hans climbed up the mast but could see nothing except the open sea.

Three hours pass. The noise sounds like a waterfall. I tell my uncle it must be a waterfall. He shakes his head, but I feel certain that I am right. Are we running towards some great waterfall, which will carry us very suddenly a few thousand feet nearer the centre of the earth? The professor, no doubt, would like this, but as for myself——

Whatever it is, there must be a few miles away something making a great noise, for now we can hear a violent roaring sound. Does it come from the sea or from the sky? I look up towards the sky—if we can call the roof of our cave the sky. The clouds above us are quiet. I see nothing there.

Then I turn to the sea, which, too, is quiet and clear. But if this noise comes from a waterfall, and if the water of our sea is going to fall and join the water of some sea lower down, the water round us should be moving more and more quickly all the time. But, so far as I can notice, the water is not moving more quickly. It seems as calm as ever.

About four o'clock Hans gets up and climbs to the top of the mast. There seems to be something that interests him.

"He can see something," said my uncle.

"I think so, too," I said.

Hans came down. He pointed to the south and said:
"*Der nere.*"

"Down there," said my uncle. He looked carefully and for a long time at the place to which Hans had pointed.

"Yes," he said.

"What can you see?"

"I can see a great stream of water shooting up out of the sea."

"Is it another terrible animal?"

"Perhaps."

"Then let's get away from it," I said.

" No, let us go and see what it is," answered my uncle.

I thought it must be some new animal, like the *ichthyosaurus*, shooting out water from its nose. And if we could see this, at the distance of at least thirty-six miles, it must be an immense animal, and it would be wise for us to keep away from it.

So on we went. The nearer we came to it, the higher the water shot. What animal could shoot out such a mass of water without ever stopping?

At eight o'clock in the evening we were not more than six miles away from it. We saw it. It was like a mountain. It lay in the sea as if it were an island. Was it an island or an animal? It seemed to be 6,000 feet long. Could it be an animal of this length? It did not move. It did not even float on the sea, for the waves of the sea fell against it. The water shoots up 500 feet and falls again in the form of rain. And we are running towards it.

Terrible fear took hold of me. I would go no farther. I decided even to cut the ropes. I went to my uncle.

" What is this? " I asked.

My uncle gave me no answer.

Suddenly Hans stood up, and pointed to the place where the danger was.

" *Holm*," said he.

" An island! " cried my uncle.

" An island? Only an island? " I said.

" Of course, it's nothing but an island," said my uncle, laughing.

" But the water? What is that? "

" *Geyser*," said Hans.

" Yes, no doubt a *geyser*,[1] like those in Iceland."

I was rather angry with myself for mistaking an island for an animal.

As we came nearer we saw the island more clearly. It looked very much like an immense whale, with its head standing sixty feet out of the water. At the highest point the stream of water flew up among the clouds.

[1] *Geyser:* a hot spring which throws water into the air.

"Let us go round the island," said the professor.

But we had to be very careful to keep away from the falling water, which would have sunk the raft in a moment. Hans managed to bring us safely to the other end of the island. I jumped on the rock. My uncle followed me, but Hans stayed on the raft.

The ground shook under our feet. The heat was very great. We came in sight of a small round lake out of which the *geyser* burst. From our thermometer we found that the water was 160 degrees hot. So this water must come from a burning centre. I could not help calling my uncle's attention to this fact.

"Well," said he, "what does that prove against my belief?"

"Oh, nothing," I said, seeing that he was likely to get angry again.

But I must confess that up to this time we had been very fortunate, and that, for some reason unknown to me, we have made this journey under surprising conditions of temperature. But I am certain that we must, at some time or other, get to the part where the central heat is at its highest point.

My uncle gives my name to this volcanic island, and now orders us to start on again.

We had by this time sailed over 800 miles on this underground sea, and so we must now be under England, 1,800 miles from Iceland.

Friday, August 21st. The next day we could see nothing more of the *geyser*. The wind grew stronger, and carried us farther and farther away from Axel Island. The roaring sound died away gradually.

The weather looks as if it would change before long. The air seems to be full of electricity; the clouds are slowly falling and are of a green-brown colour. It is getting darker.

"It looks like bad weather," I said.

The professor did not answer. He was in a bad temper all the time. He did not like the sea getting wider and wider as we sailed across it.

"We shall have a storm," I said. "Those clouds are pressing down on the sea as if they were going to crush it."

There was now no more wind. The raft was not moving.

"Let us take down the sail and the mast," I said. "It would be a wise thing to do."

"No!" said my uncle, angrily. "A hundred times no! Let me only see the rocks of the shore, and I do not care whether the raft is broken to pieces."

Almost as he spoke, there came a change. Rain came pouring down: there was a sudden burst of wind. The noise was terrible. It got darker and darker.

Suddenly the raft jumps upwards. My uncle is thrown down. He takes hold of a rope and sees the raft flying forward. He looks happy.

We go faster and faster. The wind is pressing against the sail. Will it break?

"The sail! the sail!" I cry, making signs to Hans to take it down.

"No," says my uncle.

"*Nej*," says Hans, gently shaking his head.

The rain is coming down like a waterfall. The storm bursts on us in all its violence. The thunder roars all the time without stopping.

Where are we going?

.   .   .   .

The night has been terrible. The storm is as violent as before. There is electricity all round us. The heat is growing greater and greater.

Monday, August 24th. The storm is just the same. It seems strange that it does not come to an end. How we need rest! We keep driving on to the south-east. We have already gone 600 miles since leaving Axel Island.

For three whole days we had not been able to say a word to each other. Even a word shouted in the ear would not be heard. My uncle came close to me and tried to speak. I could hear nothing, but I think he was trying to say, "We are lost! It is all over!"

I pointed to the sail, and made signs meaning, "Let us take it down."

My uncle made a sign meaning "yes".

At that moment a ball of fire appeared on the edge of the raft. The mast and the sail were carried away by the wind and flew up into the air.

We were nearly dead with fright. The great ball, about a foot wide, of a blue-white colour moved slowly, but turned round with great speed. It moved from place to place on the raft. Once it almost touched the box that held our gunpowder. We shall be blown to pieces! No, it went away; then came close to Hans, who looked at it calmly. Then it came towards my uncle, who lay down flat. Then it came to me and turned round and round close to my foot. I tried to pull my foot away, but I could not.

A strange smell filled the air. It hurt us to breathe it.

What is it that stops me from moving my foot? It feels

as if my foot were fastened to the raft. I understand what it is! This ball of electricity has magnetized all the iron on the raft. Our tools, our guns stick to each other; my shoes are sticking to a piece of iron that is fastened to the raft.

At last, by a violent effort, I manage to tear my foot away, just as the ball is going to strike me. At that moment the ball bursts. What a frightfully bright light! There is fire all around us. Then all is dark.

Where are we going?

13

SAKNUSSEMM AGAIN

Tuesday, August 25th. For many hours I must have been unconscious.

Are we still at sea? Yes, driving forward at a terrible speed. We have passed under England, under France, perhaps under all Europe!

.   .   .   .

But we hear a new noise. It sounds like the roar of the waves breaking on rocks——

.   .   .   .

At this point the notes that I had written during our journey on the raft come to an end.

What happened after the raft struck on the rocks I hardly know. I felt that I was thrown among the waves, and if I were not drowned or if anybody was not cut to pieces by the sharp rocks, it was because the strong arm of Hans picked me out of the water and brought me safely to the shore, where I found myself by the side of my uncle.

Then he went back to where the angry waves were breaking so that he might save some of our possessions. I could not speak. It was more than an hour before I really came back to life.

Even now the rain was falling.

Hans got some food ready, but I could not eat anything. Tired out by our three days without rest, we went to sleep.

When we woke up the next day, we found that the storm had quite passed away. It was beautiful weather. The sky and the sea were quiet.

"Well, my boy," said the professor, "I hope you slept well."

He spoke as if we were at home in the Königstrasse, and I had just come down to breakfast. Ah! if the storm had sent our raft to the east, we should have passed under Germany —under my dear town of Hamburg—perhaps under the street in which the dearest girl in the world lives. Then there would have been only 120 miles between us—but 120 miles straight up through a solid wall of rock.

These thoughts came to my mind before I answered my uncle's question.

"Well," he said, "I asked you how you slept."

"Very well," said I. "You seem very happy this morning, uncle."

"Yes, I am," he said, "very happy indeed. We have got there! "

"Got to the end of our journey? "

"No, but to the end of this terrible sea. We shall now go on again by land, and this time we shall be going downwards."

"But, uncle, may I ask you a question? "

"You may, Axel."

"How are we to get back? "

"Get back! Are you thinking of getting back before we have even got to the end of our journey? "

"No; I just wanted to know how we shall get back when the time comes."

"Oh, that will be very easy. The simplest thing in the world. Once we get to the middle of the earth, we shall discover a new road to get back to the surface again; or else we shall go back in a less interesting way by the same road as the one by which we came."

"In that case we must repair the raft."

" Of course."

" But have we enough food for this long journey? "

" We have. Hans is a clever fellow, and I am certain that he has saved most of our things. Anyhow, let's go and see."

I had a hope, which was almost a fear. It seemed to me impossible that anything on the raft could have been saved. I was wrong. When I got to the place I saw Hans among a large number of things all arranged in order on the sand. My uncle pressed his hand to show how thankful he felt. This man had been working while we had been sleeping, and had saved all the most valuable things.

It is true that there were serious losses. Our guns, for example, but these were not essential.

" Well," said my uncle, " as the guns have gone, we cannot expect to go shooting."

" But what about our instruments? "

" Here is the barometer, which is the most useful of all, and for which I would have given all the rest. With the barometer I can find out how deep we are, and when we are at the centre. Without it we might make a mistake and come out somewhere in Australia."

" And the compass? " said I.

" Here it is on the rock, and the chronometer and the thermometer. Oh! Hans is a splendid fellow! "

This was quite true. Not one of our instruments was lost. As to our tools I saw on the sand our ropes, picks and other things.

" And the food? " I asked.

" Yes, let's see the food."

The boxes in which our food was kept were lying side by side in a perfect state. We had enough to eat for four months.

" Four months! " cried the professor. " Why, we have enough to go and to come back; and with what is left I will give a grand dinner to my fellow-professors at the university."

" Now," he said, " we must fill our water bottles again. As to the raft, I advise Hans to do the best he can to repair it, although I don't at all expect to want it again."

" Why not? " I asked.

" It's an idea of mine, my boy. I don't think we shall come out where we came in."

I looked at my uncle, wondering whether he was mad.

" Let's go to breakfast," he said.

Then we had a very good meal—one of the best I have ever had in my life.

During the meal I asked my uncle how he was going to find out exactly where we were.

" Well, we cannot know exactly," he answered. " In fact it would be impossible, because during the three days' storm I could take no note of the speed or direction of our journey, but still, we can form some idea of our position."

" Let me see, now," I said. " At Geyser Island——"

" At Axel Island, my boy. Do not be ashamed of calling it by its right name."

" Very well. At Axel Island we had crossed 810 miles of sea, and we were more than 1,800 miles from Iceland."

" Just so. Now let us count four days of storm, during which our speed was certainly not less than 240 miles in the twenty-four hours."

" I think that is about right. So that will be 900 miles to add."

" Yes, the Sea of Lidenbrock must be 1,800 miles across! Do you know, Axel, it must be bigger than the Mediterranean."

" Yes, particularly if we have only gone across its width."

" Which is quite possible."

" Another strange thing," said I, " If our figures are right, the Mediterranean must be just over our heads! "

" Really! "

" Yes, because we are 2,700 miles from Reykjavik."

" That's a long way, my boy; but whether we are under the Mediterranean rather than under the Atlantic or under Turkey is a thing that we cannot decide unless we are certain that our direction did not change."

" Well, it's easy to find out, by looking at the compass."

The professor made his way towards the rock on which

Hans had arranged the instruments. He was eager and happy; he rubbed his hands as he walked! He was young again. I followed him, anxious to know whether my figures were right.

When my uncle got to the rock, he took up the compass, laid it straight and looked at the needle, which, after a few moments, stood still. My uncle looked and looked again; he rubbed his eyes, and looked again. Then he turned to me with a look of the greatest surprise on his face.

" What's the matter, uncle? "

He made a sign to me to look at the compass. I cried out in my surprise. The needle pointed to where we believed the south to be. It turned to the shore instead of to the open sea.

I shook the compass. I examined it; it was in good order. No matter which way I turned it, it kept pointing in the wrong direction.

We could only imagine that during the storm we had not noticed the change of wind that had brought the raft back to the shore which my uncle hoped he had left behind him.

No words can give any idea of my uncle's state: surprise, unbelief, anger. I never saw a man so disappointed at first or so violently angry after. After this dangerous and tiring journey, all must be done over again. We had gone backwards instead of forwards.

" What a misfortune! Everything is against me. Air, fire and water are doing all they can to stop me. Well, they shall not stop me. I will not go back. We shall see which will win: man or nature! "

I thought it time to show him the true state of things.

" Listen to me, uncle," said I, in a quiet voice. " There are some things that it is possible for man to do; there are other things that are not possible; it is useless to fight against what is impossible. We are not in a position to make another journey by sea; we cannot do 1,500 miles on a half-broken raft, with a piece of rug for a sail and a piece of wood for a mast. We have no oar. A storm can do what it likes with us; we are helpless."

I spoke in this way for about ten minutes, but this was

only because the professor was taking no notice of me. He did not hear a word of what I was saying.

"To the raft!" he cried.

That was his answer. I prayed to him to change his mind. It was useless. I spent my strength in fighting against a will harder than rock. Hans had just finished repairing the raft. It was as if he had guessed what my uncle meant to do. With some new pieces of this same wood, he had made the raft stronger. He had already put up a new mast and sail.

The professor gave a few orders to our guide, who at once put all our things on the raft, and got everything ready for a start. The weather was fairly clear, and there was a good wind from the north-west.

What could I do? How could I alone have any success against these two? Impossible, even if Hans were on my side. But the Icelander seemed to have no will of his own. I could do nothing with a servant who always obeyed his master. There was nothing to do except to go on. So I was just going to take my usual place on the raft when my uncle put out his hand to stop me.

"We shall not start until tomorrow," said he. "As we have been thrown on this part of the coast, I will not leave it without examining it."

We had, of course, come back to the north coast, but not to the part from which we had started. So there was nothing unreasonable in the professor's wish to examine this new part carefully.

"Let us go, then," I said.

There was some distance between the shore and the rocky wall that stood up behind. We walked for half an hour before we reached the foot of the hills. There were signs that this had once been the true sea coast. We walked along this old coast looking at everything with the greatest atten-tion. The professor thought that there might be some opening.

After a time the rocks came to an end, and we saw in front of us a wide stretch of flat country. It was covered with bones. We examined them. The history of the life on the world was spread out before us. The bones were those of animals that no longer lived on the earth.

Try to imagine our wild excitement. My uncle threw his arms up; his mouth was wide open; his head moved up and down, and from right to left, so great was his surprise.

For another half-hour we walked over this mass of bones, finding new wonders at every step. We were now some distance from the sea. One strange thing I noticed as we walked: we had no shadows! The light, which was very strong, seemed to come from nowhere in particular.

After walking about a mile farther we found ourselves on the edge of a forest, this time not of mushrooms. The trees all belonged to past ages, but they had no colour. The leaves had no greenness, and the flowers were all grey. My uncle walked into this forest, and I followed him, not without fear. For if we saw here the trees and plants of the past, why should we not see some of the terrible animals of the past, as well?

Suddenly I came to a stop. I held my uncle back. The light made everything perfectly clear even in the depth of this forest. I thought I saw—yes! I did see an immense shape moving under the trees! It was a great elephant covered with long hair. It was a *mammoth*![1] the elephant of the age of ice! And there was another, and another, and another. There must have been over twenty of them. They were tearing down the branches of the trees as they moved on.

"Come," said my uncle, "let us get nearer and have a good look at them."

"No," said I, "it is too dangerous. We have no guns. What could we do to save ourselves if these mammoths caught sight of us? No man would dare go anywhere near them."

"No man?" said my uncle. "You are mistaken, Axel. Look over there! I think I can see a man! A man like ourselves!"

I could not believe it, but I looked. It was true. About

[1] *Mammoth:* very large elephant-like animal of the past.

a quarter of a mile away, resting himself against the branch of a tree, was a man! But "he who takes care of big things must be bigger himself". And this man, who was taking care of the mammoths, was at least twelve feet high. His hair looked as wild and long as the hair of these elephants.

We stood there as if we had been turned into stone. We might be seen. We must go, and go quickly.

"Come, come!" I cried, pulling my uncle along with me, and my uncle, for the first time in his life, allowed himself to be pulled along.

A quarter of an hour later we were out of sight, and safe.

Now that I think of it all quietly; now that my mind is calm again, and that months have passed since then, what am I to think? What am I to believe? It seems impossible. Our eyes must have shown us something that was not there. No men could possibly be living down below without knowing anything of the world above.

Anyhow, we ran—ran like madmen. We found our way back to the Sea of Lidenbrock.

Although I was certain that this was not the part of the country from which we had started our journey in the raft, I often noticed groups of rocks that I seemed to have seen before. It was all very strange and difficult to believe. Hundreds of streams fell from the rocks and ran into the sea. I thought I saw the Hansbach, and the cave in which I had become conscious after my fall.

My uncle could understand nothing, either.

"Well, at least," I said, "we have not landed at the point from which we started. The storm has brought us farther down, and if we follow the shore, we shall come to our starting-point."

"If that is so," said my uncle, "we need go no farther. The best thing we can do is to get back to the raft. But are you sure you are right, Axel?"

"It is difficult to be certain, uncle," I said. "All the rocks look so much alike. And yet I seem to recognize the place where Hans made our raft."

"No, Axel. If that were so, we should see signs of our

having been here before, and I see nothing of the sort."

"But I see something!" I said, running towards something that was lying on the sand.

"What is it?"

"Look!" said I.

And I showed my uncle the knife that I had picked up.

"Axel," said my uncle, "did you bring this knife with you?"

"I? No. But you——"

"No. I certainly did not bring it. I have never had such a knife."

"How strange!"

"Well, no! After all, it's simple enough, Axel. The Icelanders often have knives of this sort. Hans must have brought it with him and dropped it here. No doubt it is his."

I shook my head. Hans never had anything of the sort.

"Axel," said my uncle, "it was not brought here by you, by Hans or by me. It has been lying here for three hundred years. Somebody has been here before us. He has somewhere cut his name on a rock with this knife! He wanted to mark once more the road to the central point! Let us look everywhere!"

We walked along the high wall of rock, looking at every crack that might be the beginning of a new passage. At last we came to a place where the sea came up as far as the rocky wall. Between two pieces of rock that were sticking out we saw the mouth of a dark passage.

There, on the rock, stood the letters that we had seen before:

"A. S.!" cried my uncle, "Arne Saknussemm! Always Arne Saknussemm!"

Since the beginning of our travels I had been surprised so often that I thought that nothing could surprise me any more. But when I saw these two letters, cut three hundred years ago, I stood there in a state of surprise that was rather near madness. Not only had the great traveller cut his name there, but in my hands was the thing he had cut it with! Then it was true after all!

While these thoughts were going through my mind the professor was talking, as if to Arne Saknussemm himself. "Wonderful man!" he cried. "You forget nothing which might serve as a guide to others who would wish to follow you. You have done everything to make it possible to follow you. Your name, cut in the rock, from place to place, shows us where and how to follow you. I believe I shall find your name cut into the rock at the centre of the earth. Well, I, too, will write my name there."

That is what I heard my uncle say, and my own excitement was growing greater at every moment. A fire seemed to be burning inside me. I forgot everything. I forgot the dangers of the journey, and the dangers of the return. What another man had done, I would dare to do, and nothing seemed to me impossible.

"Forward! forward!" I cried.

As I spoke I jumped forward towards the dark passage, when the professor, usually the first to do things in haste, said:

"Stop, Axel; we must first go back to Hans, and bring the raft round to this point."

I obeyed, and made haste to get back.

"Uncle," I said, "do you know that all sorts of accidental things have been very fortunate for us?"

"Do you think so, Axel?"

"I do. Why, everything, even the storm, helped to put us on the right road. What a splendid thing that storm was! It brought us to the coast from which fine weather would have carried us away. Just suppose that we had reached the south shore of the Lidenbrock Sea, what would have happened? We should never have seen the name of Saknussemm, and we should have been going up and down a shore without any opening to it."

"Yes, Axel, it is as if something wonderful has been guiding us on our way; something which brought us, who were going to the south, back to the north. It is more than surprising, and I cannot understand it."

"What does it matter?" I said. "It is not necessary for

us to understand how we have been guided, but only to make the best use of our good fortune."

"Certainly, my boy, but——"

"But we are going to the north again. We shall pass under the northern countries of Europe instead of going under Africa."

"Yes, Axel, you are right, and it is the best thing that could happen, as we shall be leaving this sea, which can take us nowhere. We shall go down, down, always down! Do you know that we have only 4,500 miles to travel?"

"Only 4,500 miles?" said I. "That's nothing. Let's start at once!"

We talked in this mad way until we got back to the raft. Everything was ready for us to start off at once. We took our places on the raft, put up the sail, and Hans took us along the coast.

At about six o'clock in the evening we reached the opening of the passage. I jumped on shore, followed by the professor and the Icelander.

"Let's start!" I cried.

"Yes," said my uncle, "but not before we have examined this new passage, even if only to see whether we should get our ladders ready."

The opening was about five feet across. This, then, was the passage that was going to lead us to the centre of the earth. Would it go down steeply at once? Would it be again a sort of chimney going straight down? Or should we have to spend many hours, days, or weeks without getting any nearer to the centre of the earth? We soon got an answer to these questions: sooner than we had expected!

We had not gone more than six steps when we found in front of us an immense rock putting a sudden and most unexpected end to the passage. We looked to the left, to the right; above and below. There was no doubt about it; this passage, which was going to lead us 4,500 miles down to the centre of the earth, was only twenty feet long, and then came to an end.

I was terribly disappointed. I refused to believe facts. I

bent down to look under the rock. There was not even a crack. Above, it was the same. Hans threw the light of his lamp all along the wall, but found nothing to help us. What was to be done? Was there nothing except to give up all hope of passing?

I sat down on the ground. My uncle walked up and down the short passage.

"What did Saknussemm do?" I asked.

"Ah, yes!" said my uncle, "was he stopped by this rock?"

"No! no!" I cried with warmth. "This rock must have shut up this passage since the time when Saknussemm passed this way. Many years have passed since. Saknussemm found the way open; we have found it closed. We must open it again. If we do not or cannot, we are not good enough men to reach the centre of the earth!"

"Well," said my uncle, "with the pick we must cut our way. Let us break down this wall."

"It's too hard for the pick. What about the gunpowder?"

"Gunpowder, of course," said my uncle. "Let us blow up this rock. Hans, bring the gunpowder."

The Icelander went back to the raft, and came back with a pick with which we could make a hole to put the powder in. The hole had to be big enough to hold fifty pounds of gunpowder.

I was in a state of great excitement.

"We shall pass," I said.

"We shall," said my uncle.

At twelve o'clock at night we had finished. The powder was put in.

"Let us wait until tomorrow," said the professor.

Tomorrow? It was now I who was the impatient one, and my uncle the one who was wanting to wait. There was nothing to be done. I had to agree to wait six long hours.

14

IN A VOLCANO

THE next day, Thursday, the 27th of August, was a day not to be forgotten. From that moment our reasoning and judgement were to count as nothing. We could do nothing except trust ourselves to the care of air, fire and water.

At six o'clock we were ready.

We had made a match that would take ten minutes to burn from end to end.

I asked to be the one to light this match. When I had done so, I was to join my companions on the raft. We were then to go some distance away and wait for the explosion.

My uncle and Hans went on the raft. I stayed on the shore.

"Go now, my boy," said my uncle, "and when you have done your work, come back to us at once."

"You may be quite certain, uncle, that I shall not stop on the way."

I went to the opening of the passage and took up the end of the match. The professor was holding his chronometer in his hand.

"Ready!" he cried.

"Ready!" I answered, and then lit the match. I stayed long enough to see that it was burning properly, and then ran back to the raft, on which I took my place.

Hans sent the raft out about a hundred feet from the shore. The professor looked at the chronometer.

"Five minutes more!" he said. "Four! Three!"

It was an exciting moment.

"Two! One—— Now, you rocks, fall!"

What happened? I do not think I heard the explosion. But the shape of the rocks seemed to change in front of my eyes; they opened; they opened still more; an enormous hole seemed to be opening on the shore. The sea shook, and formed one great wave. The raft was caught up on the side of this wave.

We were all three thrown down. In a moment we were in complete darkness. The water was carrying us into the hole. I thought we were going to be shot down a waterfall. I tried to speak to my uncle, but the roaring of the water made it impossible for my voice to be heard. Along and along we were carried at a mad speed.

In spite of the darkness and my fear, I understood what had happened. On the other side of the rock that we had blown up there was a deep hole, and the sea was rushing down into this hole carrying us with it to the centre of the earth.

An hour passed; two hours—who knows how many hours —passed in this way? We kept close together, holding each other's hands so as not to be thrown off the raft. We felt shocks of great violence when the raft touched the wall, but as this did not happen often I supposed that the passage was getting wider. This was certainly the road followed by Saknussemm, but instead of going down it alone, we were bringing the whole sea with us.

We were travelling much faster than the fastest train.

Our electric lamp had broken at the moment of the explosion. My surprise then was great when I saw a light shining beside me. Hans had succeeded in lighting an oil lamp. The passage was a wide one, as I had thought. The weak light did not allow us to see both walls at a time.

My uncle and I looked at each other with anxious faces as we held on to what was left of the mast, which had been broken at the time of the explosion. We turned our backs to the direction in which we were going; in this way we were able to breathe.

The hours passed.

Then we made a most unpleasant discovery; most of our possessions had gone. I wanted to know how much was left, and what it was. So with the lamp in my hand I made a thorough examination of the things on the raft. Of our instruments nothing was left except the compass and the chronometer. The only rope we had was the little that was fastened to what was left of the mast. No tools at all, not even a pick. And what was worse, we had food enough for only one day. What a terrible thought! And yet, after all, what did it matter? Suppose we had enough food to last for months, how were we to escape from this dark passage or the water that was shooting us down it? Why should I be afraid of hunger when death in so many other shapes was so near? Why, we should probably not have time to die of hunger!

Was there any possibility of our even getting back to the surface of the earth? There seemed to be no possibility at all.

I thought of telling my uncle, and showing him how little food we had. But I did not.

At that moment the light of the lamp began to grow weaker, and then suddenly went out. We were again in complete darkness.

A long time passed, and then it seemed that we were travelling faster than ever. The hill of water became steeper and steeper. Suddenly I felt a shock. The raft had not struck anything solid, but it suddenly stopped. Water was falling on us. I was drowning! But this sudden fall of water did not last long. In a few moments I was taking in long breaths of pure air.

I suppose it was now ten o'clock at night.

I suddenly noticed that there was no more noise. The roaring of the water had stopped. At last I heard my uncle speak. He said:

" We are going up! "

" What do you say? " I cried.

" I say we are going up! "

It was true. We were going up at a great speed.

" Now for the lamp. Can we light it again? "

Yes, it was now possible to light it.

" Just as I thought," said the professor. " We are in a sort of well chimney less than twenty-four feet across. The water, having got to the bottom, is now, naturally, going up again, and we are going with it."

" Where to? "

" I don't know, but we must be ready for anything. We are going up at the rate of twelve feet a second—let us say, 720 feet a minute, or nine and a half miles an hour."

" How long shall we go on like this? " I asked. " And has the well any opening at the top? If not, we shall be crushed by the weight of the air."

" Axel," said my uncle, very calmly, " our position is certainly a terrible one; but it is not a hopeless one. We may be killed at any moment, but at any moment we may be saved. So let us be ready to help ourselves if there is any possibility of doing so."

" How can we do so? "

" We can, at any rate, make ourselves stronger by eating."

At these words, I looked at my uncle with an unhappy face.

" Eat? " said I.

" Yes, at once."

The professor added some words in Danish.

Hans shook his head.

" What! " said my uncle. " Our food is lost? "

" Yes, there is all we have left—a piece of dried meat for the three of us."

My uncle looked at me hopelessly.

" Well," said I, " do you still think we may be saved? "

My question received no answer.

An hour passed. I was suffering from hunger. My companions were suffering, too; but none of us would touch the little food that was left.

We kept going up very quickly. The air was getting hotter. What did this mean?

I said to the professor:

" If we are neither drowned nor crushed, and if we do not die of hunger, there is still the possibility that we shall be burnt to death."

The professor did not answer.

An hour passed, and there was no change, except that it kept getting warmer.

At last my uncle said:

"Come! we must eat. If we save the little food that we have so as to give us a few more hours of life, we shall make ourselves weaker at the end."

"Yes, at the end. That will be very soon. When that piece of meat has gone, what have we?"

"Nothing, Axel, nothing."

"Then you are without hope?"

"You are wrong; I am full of hope. We are still alive, and while there's life there's hope!"

Who except my uncle could say a thing like that!

"Well," I said, "what is your plan?"

"To eat what is left, and get back our lost strength. It may be our last meal, it is true, but at least it will give us strength to meet the end."

"Very well," I said.

My uncle took the food that was left, and divided it into three equal parts. That gave about a pound to each of us. The professor ate well and quickly. In spite of my hunger I ate with difficulty and without any pleasure. Hans ate calmly and quietly.

Our last meal came to an end. We felt better and stronger. It was now five o'clock in the morning.

Each of us was thinking his own thoughts. What was Hans thinking about? Who knows? As for me, my thoughts were nothing but memories, and they carried me to the surface of the earth, which I should never have left. They carried me to the home in the Königstrasse, my dear Gräuben, our good Martha.

My uncle, always busy, was examining the rocks. He was trying to find out where we were by noticing what they were and how they were arranged.

"We are still very far down," he said. "But we are still going up."

I could not help feeling rather amused to notice the change in my uncle. We were going up—and he was happy.

Only a short time ago, the only thing that made him happy
was going down.

It was getting hotter and hotter.

"Uncle," I asked, "are we getting near burning rocks?"

"No," said my uncle, "it is impossible."

"And yet," said I, touching the wall, "this rock is hot."

As I spoke, my hand touched the water, and I took it out
very quickly.

"The water is boiling hot."

This time the professor answered only by an angry movement. From that moment I became more and more
frightened. I expected at any moment some terrible happening. What it would be I did not know; I could not put
it into words.

I looked at the compass; the needle was not still for a
moment; it kept turning round and round. Then I heard
sounds like distant explosions. I looked at the beds of rock
through which we were passing, and it seemed to me that
they sometimes shook. These walls of rock were going to
move in and crush us to death.

"Uncle! Uncle!" cried I, "there is no hope!"

"What new fear has taken hold of you now?" he
answered, with surprising calmness. "What's the matter
with you now?"

"What's the matter with me? Look at these moving walls;
look at this hot water, feel this terrible heat—every sign
of an earthquake!"

My uncle only shook his head gently.

"An earthquake?" said he.

"Yes."

"My boy, I think you are mistaken."

"What! You don't notice the signs?"

"Of an earthquake? No! I expect something better than
that!"

"What do you mean?"

"I mean a volcano, Axel."

"A volcano!" said I. "Then we are in the middle of an
active volcano!"

"Yes, I think so," said the professor, smiling. "And per·
haps that's the best thing that could happen to us."

The best thing! Was my uncle mad? What could he
mean? Why this unnatural smiling calmness?

"What?" said I. "We are caught in a volcano; we have
been thrown into a chimney of burning lava, of rocks of
fire, of boiling water, of hot steam. We shall be shot up into
the air with the rocks, and you say that this is the best
thing that can happen to us!"

"Yes," said the professor, "it's our only hope of getting
to the surface again."

My uncle was right: it was certainly our only hope of
getting to the surface again.

We were still going up; the night passed. The noises
grew louder. It became almost impossible to breathe; I
thought my last hour had come.

It was clear that we were being forced upwards by an
volcanic pressure; under the raft was boiling water, and
under the water there was liquid lava that on reaching
the crater would be shot in every direction. We were in the
chimney of a volcano. There was no doubt about it.

But this time, instead of Sneffel, which was an old volcano,
we were in an active volcano. I began to wonder what mountain it was and on what part of the earth we should be
shot out.

We were, of course, in the north. Had we gone back in
the direction of Iceland? Were we to make our way out of
Hecla or by one of the seven other craters of the island?

Towards the morning we found ourselves going up still
faster. The heat got greater as we got nearer the surface.

Under us was no longer water; it was a thick mass of
liquid burning matter.

About eight o'clock something very strange happened:
we stopped.

"What is it?" I asked.

"We have come to a stop," answered my uncle.

"Is the explosion over?"

"I hope not."

I stood up. I tried to look about me. Perhaps the raft had caught on a point of rock. But no. Everything had stopped, not only the raft, but the soft liquid stuff as well.

" Be patient, my boy," said my uncle: " this calm will not last very long. Five minutes have already passed, and very soon we shall start again." As he spoke he was looking at his chronometer. He was right. Soon the raft began to move upwards again. The movement lasted two minutes, and, then we stopped again.

" Good! " said my uncle. " In ten minutes we shall start again."

" Ten minutes? "

" Yes, this is one of those volcanoes that blows up every ten minutes. It lets us take breath."

Quite true. Ten minutes later we started off again. We moved so quickly that we had to hold tight to the raft so as not to be thrown off. Then the pressure stopped again.

How often this happened I cannot say. I only know that each time we started the force was greater. The heat was growing all the time. I thought for a moment what a pleasure it would be to find ourselves among the snow and ice of the extreme north. Gradually I began to lose consciousness. Shock after shock, together with the frightful heat, had made me weak. If Hans had not taken care of me I should more than once have had my head crushed against the rock wall.

I have no very clear memory of what happened in the hours that followed. I have a general idea of a noise that never stopped, of the raft turning round and round on the lava sea that pushed it up. The roaring fire was all round it. The last thing I can remember is the face of Hans lit up by the bright red of the fire.

15

OUT OF THE VOLCANO

WHEN I became conscious again, and opened my eyes, I found myself held by the strong hand of our guide. With the other he was holding my uncle. I was not badly hurt, but only very, very tired.

I was lying on the side of a mountain two steps away from a place where the ground dropped straight down for thousands of feet. If we had made any movement we should have fallen. Hans had saved us again. Moving on hands and knees with very great care, we got to a safe place, and we could then look round us.

First, we saw that it was the real sky above our heads, and not a sky made of rock. For the first time for sixty-two days we could see the sky. So we were once more on the surface of the earth. But where?

"Where are we?" asked my uncle, who now seemed not very pleased at finding himself on the surface of the earth again.

Hans made a movement to show that he did not know.

"In Iceland?" I asked.

"*Nej!*"

"What? No?" cried the professor.

"Hans is mistaken," I said.

We had had many surprises during our journey, and this was not the least of them. We expected to see the top of a volcano covered with ice and snow, like Sneffel, in the middle of the cold northern country. But here we were on a mountain-side which was dried and burnt by the heat of the sun. I could not believe my eyes, but there was no doubt about it.

The professor was the first to speak:

"After all, it is not like Iceland. This is not a northern volcano."

Above our heads, 500 feet away at least, was the edge of the crater from which we had been thrown out. At every ten minutes, with a loud explosion, stones came flying out. I could feel the movement. Below us were the steep sides of the mountain, which seemed to be not more than 1,800 feet high. Not very far from us we could see the green of woods and gardens.

Not like Iceland, certainly.

Beyond the green woods was the blue sea. It seemed, then, that we were on a small island. To the east were a few houses. On a sea, not far, there were ships of a strange shape. Beyond these there were a large number of islands. Looking towards the south we could see a distant land on which there was a very high mountain, on the top of which there was a cloud of black smoke.

It was indeed a beautiful sight.

"Where are we? Where are we?" I kept asking myself.

Hans shut his eyes: he did not seem very interested.

My uncle said:

"Whatever mountain this is, we are in a rather warm place—and a dangerous place, too. As we have come safely through the middle of an active volcano, it seems a pity to be killed by a falling rock. Let's go down, and then we shall find out where we are. Besides, I'm dying of hunger and thirst."

The way down was very steep, and walking was not at all easy. All the time we were coming down I was talking.

"We must be in Asia," I cried, "on the shores of India, or perhaps the Malayan Islands. We have crossed half the world to come out on the other side."

"But how about the compass?" said my uncle.

"Yes, according to the compass we have been going to the north all the time."

"Then the compass did not tell us the truth!"

"Oh, uncle! Did not tell us the truth?"

I could think of no answer to this question.

And now we were near the beautiful country, I felt hungry, and thirsty too. Fortunately we came to a wood where fruit was growing which looked as if it belonged to everybody. We found water, too. With what pleasure we drank it, and washed ourselves in it.

Suddenly a child appeared among the trees.

"Ah!" I said. "There's somebody who belongs to this happy land!"

It was a poor child, with poor-looking clothes, and clearly very frightened of us.

Just as he was running away, Hans went and brought him back in spite of his cries. My uncle began by comforting him and asked him in German:

"My little friend, what is the name of this country?"

No answer.

"Very good," said my uncle, "we are not in Germany," and he asked the question in English.

No answer.

"We are not in England. Let's try Italian," said my uncle, and he asked:

"Dove noi siamo?"

No answer.

"What! you won't speak!" said my uncle, who was getting angry. He pulled the child's ears and asked, still in Italian:

"What do you call this island?"

"Stromboli," said the little boy, and ran away through the trees. But we did not need him any more.

Stromboli! What an unexpected name! So we were on an island in the middle of the Mediterranean. And the blue mountains on the east were the mountains of Calabria! And the volcano far away to the south was Etna!

What a wonderful journey we had made! In by one volcano; out by another, and this other being more than three thousand miles from Sneffel. We had left the treeless country of snow and ice and had come to one of the most beautiful countries on earth.

After a most welcome meal of fruit and water, we walked on towards the little town. We thought it wise not to tell the people there where we had come from, and how we had come. They would not understand. We would simply tell them that we were sailors and that our boat had gone down by accident.

As we walked on, I could hear my uncle saying to himself:

"But the compass—it always pointed to the north. How can we explain it?"

"Don't explain it!" said I. "That's the easiest plan."

"What an idea! A professor at the university who was not able to find an explanation of a thing like that! Impossible!"

An hour after leaving the little wood we got to Port San Vicenzo, where Hans asked to be paid for his thirteenth week of service. My uncle gave it to him with very great pleasure. At this moment our guide did something that we had never seen him do before: he smiled!

Here our story comes to an end. Nobody will ever believe it, of course. But no matter; I am used to people who refuse to believe anything that is not in agreement with the things they want to believe.

We were received by the people of Stromboli very kindly. They gave us food and clothes. On the 31st of August, after a stay of only forty-eight hours, we were able to sail for Messina, where a few days of rest made us forget how tired we had been.

On Friday, September the 4th, we left Messina by a fine French boat, and, three days later, reached Marseilles. There was only one thing that troubled us, and that was the strange way in which our compass had acted.

On September the 9th, late in the evening, we reached Hamburg.

I will not try to describe the surprise of Martha or the happiness of Gräuben.

"Now that you are a famous man," said this dear girl, "you will not want to leave me again, Axel."

The coming back of Professor Lidenbrock, I need not say, caused great excitement in Hamburg. Because of Martha's talk, everybody had heard of his journey to the centre of the earth. Nobody believed it, and now that he had come back they believed it less than ever.

Still, the fact that Hans was with us, and some news received from our friends in Iceland, made some people believe our story.

And so my uncle became a great man, and so did I. Hamburg gave a dinner of welcome to us. There was a great meeting at the university, where my uncle told the story of our journey—saying, however, nothing about the compass. On the same day he made a present to the university library of the parchment written by Saknussemm.

Of course, being so famous soon made enemies for my uncle. As his ideas agreed with facts that could be proved, and did not agree with the usual scientific beliefs (which were not proved), he was attacked by screaming men in every country.

We were made very unhappy one day when Hans told us that he had decided to go home. We asked him again and again to stay with us. We owed everything to him, our success and our lives. But he refused to take any reward. He was anxious only to return home.

"*Färval*," he said one day, and with that little word he went off to Iceland.

We had come to like this brave fellow. Although he is far away, he will never be forgotten by those whose lives he saved so many times, and I will certainly see him again before I die.

My uncle and I had become great men. All over the world our names were known; we were famous. We had done an important piece of work for science. And yet there was one thing that troubled us; it was about the compass. So long as that matter was not explained my uncle would never be happy.

One day, while I was at work in his study, this compass happened to catch my eye. It had been lying there for six months. I looked at it. What a surprise! I called out to my uncle:

"Come here!"

My uncle hurried to me.

"What is it?" he asked.

"The compass! Its needle is pointing to the south instead of the north!"

"Impossible!" cried my uncle.

"Look at it!" I answered.

"Well then," said he, "at some time when we were on the Sea of Lidenbrock, the needle of this compass came to point to the south instead of to the north."

"Clearly."

"Then our mistake is explained. What could have caused the change?"

"I think I can tell you that," said I. "During that storm on the Sea of Lidenbrock, that ball of fire that magnetized all the iron on the raft magnetized the compass as well."

My uncle laughed. "Then it was a joke, an electrical joke!"

From that day my uncle was the happiest of men—except perhaps myself. For Gräuben was now my wife.

QUESTIONS

CHAPTER 1

1. How did the professor show his impatience (a) when teaching (b) in his walk (c) with his plants?
2. At what else, besides geology, was he clever?
3. Describe the book that the professor brought home.
4. How did he know that the writing on the parchment was much later than that in the book?
5. What did he find on the back of the first page?
6. Explain (a) Runic (b) parchment (c) cryptogram.
7. What was Axel's secret?
8. Mention some of the troubles caused by dinner.

CHAPTER 2

1. In what language was the cryptogram written?
2. How did Axel find the right way to read it?
3. Why was he afraid to tell his uncle the truth?
4. How did he try to end the matter, and why did he fail?
5. Give two reasons why Axel told his uncle the truth.
6. What was the secret in the message?
7. Act the scene beginning on page 18 at "The professor got up" and ending on page 20 at "into the dining-room".

CHAPTER 3

1. Show that the professor was really pleased with Axel.
2. Why did he want to keep the journey a secret?
3. "Science is always changing as new facts are discovered." Do you know any examples of this?
4. Give two reasons why Axel thought it impossible to go down the crater. What answers did his uncle make?
5. On what idea did the professor and Sir Humphrey Davy agree?
6. Why did Axel go out?
7. What made him feel that he must go with his uncle after all?
8. Why was the professor in such a hurry to start?

CHAPTER 4

1. What was Gräuben's promise when she said good-bye?
2. Mark, in red, on the map on page 36, the journey from Hamburg to Reykjavik.
3. When did (a) Axel (b) his uncle feel sick?
4. What reminded Axel of the madness of their journey?

5. Who welcomed the professor and his nephew at Reykjavik?
6. Where, in the town, did they stay?
7. How did most of the people earn their living?
8. Why did the professor visit (a) the Copenhagen museum (b) the Reykjavik library?

CHAPTER 5

1. Why were there only a few uninteresting books to be seen in the Reykjavik library?
2. Why did Arne Saknussemm put his secret into a cryptogram?
3. Why was a guide needed to reach Sneffel?
4. Compare Hans and the professor.
5. How long is (a) a Danish mile (b) an English mile?
6. Which of the things they took with them, would be useful for the actual descent into the volcano?
7. What are the good qualities of Icelandic horses?

CHAPTER 6

1. Describe the struggle between the professor and his horse. Which won?
2. Why did they have to wait to cross the water?
3. Show that the Icelandic family was poor.
4. " When science has spoken, it is not for us to say anything." Find, on page 23, an opposite statement to this.
5. Was there more or less land on the earth, millions of years ago?
6. Why was the dust storm dangerous?

CHAPTER 7

1. Which part of America could be seen from Sneffel?
2. What made the crater unsafe in places?
3. What showed that Arne Saknussemm had really been down the crater?
4. Why did the bad weather make the professor angry?
5. Show how they got down 2,800 feet with a 400 feet rope.
6. Who carried the scientific instruments?
7. What did they find at the bottom of the chimney?

CHAPTER 8

1. What was the chief difficulty in getting along the first passage?
2. When did the professor expect to find water?
3. Give three reasons why Axel thought that they had chosen the wrong new passage.
4. How did the professor show that he loved his nephew?
5. What agreement did he make with Axel?

CHAPTER 9

1. How did Hans help them?
2. What was unexpected about the water?
3. Why could they not stop up the water-hole?
4. How deep in the earth were they when they came to the great hole?
5. What made it easy to go down the hole?
6. How long, at their present rate, would it take them to get to the centre of the earth?
7. What effect did the heavy air have on (*a*) the ears (*b*) breathing?

CHAPTER 10

1. What made Axel lose his companions?
2. What happened to (*a*) the stream (*b*) the passage (*c*) the lamp?
3. What, did Axel think, caused the loud noise? What really caused it?
4. Where did the voices come from?
5. Why did Axel not use his own watch to note the time?
6. How far away was his uncle?
7. Did Hans show any feeling when he saw that Axel was alive?

CHAPTER 11

1. What made Axel think, when he woke up, that they were on the surface of the earth again?
2. How had Axel been nearly killed?
3. What sort of trees were there in the forest?
4. Under what part of the world was the cavern?
5. Of what was the raft made?
6. Mention all the things they saw, besides the sea, that seemed like natural parts of the earth's surface.

CHAPTER 12

1. Why did the professor become dissatisfied?
2. What did they see when Hans drew the pick out of the water?
3. Why would the guns be useless?
4. What saved the travellers from the sea animals?
5. Describe the different creatures that lived in the Sea of Lidenbrock.
6. What caused the heat and the strange noise?
7. Why could not Axel move his foot on the raft?

CHAPTER 13

1. How did Hans help when the raft struck the rocks?
2. In what ' easy ' way did the professor expect to return to the surface of the earth

3. How much food had they left?
4. Why could they not know their position exactly any more?
5. What was strange about the compass?
6. Describe what they saw in the forest.
7. Whose knife did they find?
8. What stopped them in the new passage, and how did they plan to open it?

CHAPTER 14

1. What happened to the raft when the explosion took place?
2. What was lost from the raft?
3. How did each person make his last meal?
4. What signs showed they were in an active volcano?
5. Why was the professor pleased?
6. What took the place of water under them?
7. Why did the raft keep stopping and starting again?

CHAPTER 15

1. Describe the scene they saw when they got to the surface of the earth.
2. How did they find out where they were?
3. What made some people believe the traveller's story?
4. What was the explanation of the strange behaviour of the compass?

GENERAL QUESTIONS

1. Compare Iceland and the Icelanders with your own country and people.
2. What do you learn from the story about life on the earth millions of years ago?
3. Which, do you think, was the most dangerous part of the adventure? Describe it.
4. What and where were (*a*) the Hansbach (*b*) the Sea of Lidenbrock (*c*) Axel Island?